A. R. Leonard

Unconditional Counsel

God's counsel is
the wisest counsel

Printed in the United States of America.

Imprint: Nita Nae's Books – Truthful Imagination, 2025

Publishing & Distribution: CFP, 2020/ Revised Lulu.com, 2025

ISBN 979-8-9923146-4-9 (paperback)

Arnita R. Leonard

Unconditional Counsel © 2018

Nita Nae's Books – Truthful Imagination © 2015

4859 W. Slauson Avenue, Ste. A - #354

Los Angeles, CA 90056

What Others Are Saying About
Unconditional Counsel

"This is a book that shows the power of prayer and having a true relationship with God."

—*L. Howard*

"I enjoyed Erica's story—how she recognized she needed changing and allowed God to work. The characters were very realistic. I was so drawn in. I truly felt like I was reading about someone's life."

—*L. Jackson*

"Unconditional Counsel is relatable, powerful, and entertaining. It depicts the journey of a woman who has learned to discern the difference between love and lust based on her personal experiences, and God's grace and mercy. Love it!"

—*M. Johnson*

"This book it's too hard to put down, every event makes you want to see what's going to happen next. It is captivating and a reflection of real-life situations."

—*S. Hart*

Unless otherwise noted, all Bible Scriptures are taken from the King James Version of the Holy Bible.

Unconditional
Counsel

A. R. Leonard

Acknowledgments

To God be the glory for all He has done in my life. For without Him, I can do nothing. I thank God for trusting me with this gift and allowing me to pay it forward for others to walk this path and journey as I learn to navigate these waters called writing and publishing. I never thought I would end in this place of…Truthful Imagination.

I want to dedicate this book to my late Uncle Alvin and Aunt Mamie. My Great-Uncle was such a humble example of salvation. My Great-Aunt did the work God called her to do for His righteousness.

To my sons David and Joshua, for the loving support I needed. To my dad and late mom, Otis and Margo Leonard, and the rest of my family in Denver/Aurora, Colorado. Love you much.

I want to give a shout out to all my Greater Deliverance Family in Inglewood. Love you all to life.

To three special ladies who have always had my back, my front, my mind, and my heart no matter where you were—Sister Patricia Luke, Pastor Jackie, and Evang. Lynnette (my BFF). I love you all very much.

I also want to thank Maria Johnson-Robinson for encouraging me to follow my dream. Thanks to Chontali Herod-Kirk for all her hard work editing my initial version. Thank you, Mr. Katzman (my High School English Teacher), for planting the seed and thirty-two years later still giving me pointers to improve my craft.

Thank you to all others who have helped me with this project (my Beta Readers). Without your support, I would have never achieved a completed book.

Contents

Prologue

The Why of the Revision?

To the Reader: The reason for this revision is to provide the best writing I can and to examine where I can improve. I spent many years mulling over hundreds of drafts of this book. This revision is only a part of my learning and growth as a writer and ferocious editor.

In the spirit of excellence, I wanted to revise *Unconditional Counsel* so that it flows better and to be in line with the sequel *Unconditional Counsel 2: Fate Unbroken*, when it's completed. I wanted to make sure I offered the readers the best versions possible.

As I continue my writing journey, I also came across the fact that a few companies can deplete your funds when you enlist their services for your book, Vanity Presses. I didn't want to continue to pay them money to keep my book in their rotation, and then pay them an arm and a leg to revise it. I loved the work they did on my book throughout the entire season it was in their possession. I trust my one book would not hurt their business if I went out on my own.

So, having said all of that, I hope you enjoy this updated version and also consider purchasing its sequel!

Unconditional Counsel was the 3rd novel I wrote. In my late twenties, I learned a thing or two about myself. This book allowed me to heal along the way in and from brokenness. I intertwined my life within the chapters and I enjoyed using my imagination to twist and turn the characters in an authentic way.

The scriptures are authentic and I employed them to aid others in comprehending that even in the most difficult of times, God has a plan and a word to guide you through any situation. *Unconditional Counsel* has divorce, love, lust, marriage, mystery, and murder within the pages. It is through your imagination that you can possibly discern which parts of this story are mine. ENJOY!

Chapter 1

Broken Beginnings

I DESPISE YOU", rang from Erica's lips as her soon-to-be ex-husband informed her about his plans to move in with another woman. She could do nothing but feel hurt and harbor a deep dislike of his existence that still lingered in this world. There was no chance of them getting back together, but that news was a blow to her heart. She acknowledged within the enduring love for him, but he no longer felt the same towards her. It was clear from this confirmation that this other woman was the catalyst for the divorce. Leaving a 'Dear John' letter was the initial slap in the face, and now he was doing it again.

Marrying young was not beneficial for either one of them. Immaturity was not found on either side. Erica wanted the fantasy of being a wife and mother and staying home with the children. He wanted the fantasy of having a hoochie-momma for a wife. Both of their parents were still married to each other but they never took the time to learn how to be a wife or a husband to each other. It was a matter of time before their lives would implode but Erica never thought he would cheat. They both never received what each other could offer of their true selves.

"How dare you bring this up to me!"

"I wanted to tell you because of our son. She, too, will be involved in his life," he said.

"Not if I have any say in the matter."

See, they had only separated a couple of months prior. They almost got back together once during those two months, but those embers of betrayal crept back in, and this was the final straw. Her life was spiraling out of control; trying to keep it together in front of everyone else—especially him. She was dying inside. Erica felt like he had tossed aside all the time, forgiveness, and energy she had put in. What was she going to do now? She was a babe in Christ—would she get the last laugh in this scenario without losing who she was or her faith?

The combination of love and hate was a result of the deep hurt he caused. They were supposed to be together forever, till death did them part. And that's what she wanted for him or her to be dead.

> *How could I not see it? It was impossible for me to overlook the fact that I felt broken. I hadn't been myself for a very long time. The enemy had me bound. I wore blinders and lived in denial because I didn't want to believe the truth. The truth is, I was lost in mind, and spirit. I rolled along like everything was okay, but how much could I take before being broken got the better of me? Here is where you will learn my story.* –Erica Manning

~

Five years later, Erica tried her best to be a good Christian. She threw around her faith like a badge of honor and tried hard to live a godly life. Every morning, before having to wake up her children for school, she would linger in bed and muster up enough faith to say a brief prayer. Erica would thank God for allowing her to see another day. She prayed God would protect her children and the angels would watch over them. She cried often because she felt like she had failed God and had done little to honor Him. "I hate myself", was all she could hear within her heart and mind. Erica was pretty. Her skin was a caramel shade and her face was blemish-free. The only thing that this five-foot nine, near-flawless woman ever had to correct was a set of crooked teeth, and she had those fixed with braces when she was sixteen years old. There was nothing wrong with her physically, but that didn't stop the doubting.

~

Erica had since been in a couple of relationships before and after the divorce was final. She needed a man in her life. Gary was the man who presented well. He was polished, a military man, and charming. He understood the ramification of his choices, but had no man, but the military to show him what a man was supposed to be. He grew up with his mom and grandmother because his dad died when he was six, and his grandfather before he was twelve. He longed for a loving relationship and there was no shortage of women he could have been with. He graduated with a bachelor's degree before deciding to go full-time into the military. They both were looking for each other, and friendship ensued after meeting at a Jazz concert in Leimert Park. He often thought about marriage, it wasn't until Erica, he decided to take that plunge.

"Erica, I know we've been friends for some time now, but I was wondering if it could be more?"

"We do well as friends, Gary."

"But… what's making you hesitate?"

"I'm just wondering if we want the same thing."

"We won't know if we don't try and talk about it."

~

Now married again, the man whom Erica loved rose from the bed they shared and asked her to press his pants for a business meeting he had that afternoon. As an IT specialist, Gary had to go after new clients constantly. Erica pressed Gary's pants without hesitation or reservation because she loved him and knew that he needed her.

Without saying goodbye, Gary went off to the gym. 'That was okay', Erica thought. But was it really? She reasoned that it was, in fact, okay for him to leave without saying goodbye, because this morning was peaceful. Normally, she would wake up cringing to see what kind of mood he was in, and she constantly walked on eggshells, because…

why start the day on edge when you don't have to. If he woke up and said, "Good morning," then she knew everything was okay and he wasn't mad about anything.

Most mornings Gary woke up on the wrong side of the bed, and arguments would fill the air. Erica was always the one he blamed for the arguments, which occurred ninety percent of the time over something the boys did or didn't do. If Gary fell silent and slammed the door when he left, she knew not to say anything when he returned home. But this morning was peaceful, and it made her feel better than usual.

The morning dew swept across Erica's black, ankle-high boots as she watered the windows of her car to get rid of the frost. While standing there, she wondered what the day would bring. Would it bring joy, pain, or sorrow? Maybe some happiness? Lately, these thoughts were routine. It was as if she had no clue what her purpose was in life. 'What else is there to live for but my children?' she often thought.

When these thoughts would come, she reminded herself she was here to love her three boys. 'What else is left but to live for my children?' she thought. After all, she loved her children more than she loved herself. Her mind was in a strange place, and though it was hard for her to get through each day, she tried to trust God with her life to keep from going insane.

Riding down Figueroa every morning was a part of Erica's normal routine, but this morning was different. Her car was running badly. She had known for a while that it was time to buy a new one, but because of bills like the mortgage and her children's private school tuition, she could not afford to get that brand-new Bentley which would have looked so beautiful in her driveway.

The ladies of the night were no longer visible on the streets, and the traffic was heavier than usual. Finally, merging from the 110N to the 101W – Hollywood freeway, Erica exited the Sunset Boulevard ramp to reach her regular weekday destination. Though her car was running badly, it got her to work safely.

Erica sat at her desk bored, thinking on how grateful she was to have a job in these trying times. She had been doing administrative work for ten years and desperately needed a change. Although she loved her job because of the flexible hours, she wasn't doing what made her happy. Journaling down things that happened on the previous day. She carried her journal with her almost everywhere and did most of her journaling at work because it was a peaceful place to write. Her office had four walls, all peach-colored, and she had a view of the terrace where people would smoke and have fifteen-minute conversations about work and their personal lives. Her back turned to the window to start processing the day, she felt safer and more peaceful there than at home. If people weren't out on the terrace, they were in Erica's office asking her for advice. Most of them were younger than she was, but some were older. Erica counseled her co-workers about life experiences often. In fact, ever since she was in high school, Erica's peers always came to her for advice, and she never hesitated to help them find the answers to their problems.

When Erica was younger, she dreamed of having a career in counseling, but she could never find the time to attend college. Now that she was older, she had more time, but doubted she would ever get accepted into a university. Still, she applied, but discouragement set in after the university rejected her application. Despite her doubt, Erica was not a quitter and she would try again. There was something aloof about Erica counseling her peers. She could help others, but she could not help herself. What made her own struggles so difficult to get through she could give up on herself and her self-worth so easily?

Most of the time, Erica wondered why God kept her alive at all. She had done stupid things just as others did, but she found it hard to forgive herself because the mistakes she made seemed much worse than others; in her mind, her mistakes were worse than they were in reality. Erica knew sin was sin, and there was no middle ground. The fear of sinning consumed her and decreased the joy in her life.

Growing up, it was heaven or hell. Even today, she knew that to be the case. They would put the fear of God in you, but so often it would backfire. Most kids would rebel because of the strictness of the faith. They could do nothing. No movies, no going out with boys or even going out with friends to a party. They couldn't watch television unless it was 'Leave It To Beaver'. It was to the traditional extreme that Erica so often thought about. The thing that she was missing was the knowledge of God's mercy and grace in His word.

Her children kept her going and brought joy to her each day, but she knew eventually they would grow up and be gone. They would have their own lives to live, and she wanted all of them to be successful and give her grandchildren someday. She prayed that her future grandchildren would not come soon, and that her children would wait to have them after finishing college, a good job, and marriage. Erica wanted her children to go to college right after high school, which was something she could not do.

Erica adopted her oldest son, Nolan, with her first husband, Derek. After seven years of being together, they had no children together and decided to adopt. After two years of going through the adoption process, Nolan was finally theirs, and they loved him unconditionally. But the love Erica and her husband had for each other eventually faded, and their marriage became troubled. Derek was relatively handsome, with very little baggage. At five-foot ten, he was not much taller than Erica. He had a medium build and thought he looked better than he did. Erica loved him despite their challenges and did not want their marriage to end.

They married young, which was probably the first mistake they made together. At twenty-two and twenty-four, it seemed like they were meant to be, because they knew each other since elementary school and were next-door neighbors. Their first kiss was in the backyard; they sat on a tire swinging under an avocado tree, and they kissed as a dare. Their parents expected them to marry, and they felt pressured to meet that expectation, which was the second mistake they made: trying to please everyone else.

A few years of marriage had passed, with Erica and Derek having no children to call their own. This took an emotional toll on Erica's well-being and led Derek's foot-loose and fancy-free pecker to sprout with another woman who could give him his own biological children. Erica and Derek finally divorced.

Though Erica and her son Nolan did not see eye-to-eye on many things, she loved him unconditionally. He had been born drug-exposed and struggled with his emotions. Diagnosed with ADHD, he would cry with sadness at the drop of a hat and would be just as mean and angry the next minute. Erica truly believed Nolan was one of the blessed ones. He never had to have any surgeries. At first, he had problems adjusting to regular school, but eventually, he felt comfortable and flourished in the classroom. He was truly God's blessing.

Nolan was now thirteen years old and still trying to adjust to the challenges of ADHD. He had been on medication since he was seven years old, and it seemed to help a great deal along with Erica's prayers and God's mercy. Erica was trying to adjust to the challenges as well. She had to deal with his temper-tantrums by herself. He would never have one in front of her new husband, Gary, who was the father of her two younger sons, Greg and Roderick. At age eight and four, Greg and Roderick were mischievous and full of life. God had blessed Erica's womb twice after Derek left, and the love for Nolan never ceased.

Erica's life at home with Gary was not like a typical marriage. She wanted to communicate with him more, but it was hard for her to do so. Early in their marriage, Gary was better at speaking and getting his point across. Erica felt intimidated. He'd make his points clear but would never try to bring any closure or resolution to their conversation. Most of the time, she would cry herself to sleep because none of the issues were resolved. She could talk to everyone else but Gary, and she couldn't figure out why. They had been arguing a lot more these days, and the love she felt for him was waning. It seemed like the longer they stayed married, the more they argued over things that should not have mattered.

Everything was out of sorts, and she didn't know how to fix it. Could they even fix everything if both would talk about their problems and work together to resolve the issues, misunderstandings, arguments, and compromise on the matters that count the most for each of them?

Erica's Journal Entry:

It is now 8:30 p.m., and I'm waiting for our talk. As I lie on the black leather chaise next to the triple bay window, I look up to the sky and gaze at the stars. On nights like tonight, when the sky is clear and the winds are gone, I never want to move from this spot because it is so majestic and pure, and I know God can hear me.

Gary has been standing in front of the bay window for the past fifteen minutes. He knows that I'm waiting for him, but he keeps talking on his cell phone and watering the lawn. He won't even bother to come in and say, "I'll be there when I get off the phone," or, "I'll be there when I finish watering the lawn." The impression I have is that resolving our conflict is more important to me than it is to him, so I'm going upstairs. With butterflies in my stomach, I'm praying in our room, asking God to direct my mouth and keep me from saying anything to Gary that would make this situation worse.

As I pray, I am reminded of Psalm 19:14: *"Let the words of my mouth, and the meditation of my heart, be acceptable in thy sight, O Lord, my strength, and my redeemer."* A song from my iPod is playing in the background, and the singer is singing this song: "I am God's Blessing." I wish Gary would treat me like I am God's blessing. He treats me more like a doormat, and like I am here to be used while he enjoys his life and everyone in it but me.

On this night, I have put my mouth and this situation in God's hands. My intent was for our talk to help clear the air so we could feel like a family again. The damage has already been done, but it isn't entirely my fault. I don't think our marriage is to the point of divorce or separation, but if we would just communicate better, I believe we could have it all. Maybe I just need to communicate what I need and pray he actually listens.

It's now thirty minutes later. Now I am feeling angry. I'm thinking about Ephesians 4:26, where it states: *"Be ye angry, and sin not."* I ask the Lord to take the spirit of cussing away from my mind. I really want to use some words Gary uses on me; maybe my cussing will get through to him. Back in the day, sailors had nothing on me, but I stopped that type of language a long time ago.

Gary just came in from talking to the neighbors. I hear him. I know he is going to eat first. I bet he will eat a microwaved burrito with corn chips and a soda. I just know it. And there it is. The microwave door just closed, and I can smell the chicken, cheese, and green chili. He's in the TV room. He's now sitting down, watching television, and saying nothing. He burped louder than an echo from the Grand Canyon, but still says nothing to acknowledge that we are supposed to talk tonight. Is he waiting for Roderick to go to sleep? Should I go say something? Should I even have to remind him?

My head is hurting now. Since my last marriage, I have been suffering from migraines. I don't think I should have to say anything to Gary to remind him about our talk. He was the one who scheduled it. I would not be available for the rest of this week—on purpose. I don't have any plans yet, but I'll find something to do. I just know if I say anything, he will make a smart remark or call off the talk and blame me for it. Did he really forget we were supposed to talk tonight? He's still switching the channels on the television, and the volume level is so loud! He's switching the channels over and over. He's opening up another soda. I can hear every move he makes. I hear him sucking food from his teeth. It's a disgusting sound; even more so, I am mad as hell at this point.

Gary just sent Roderick to the bedroom to see if I was awake. Roderick is looking at me now, so I asked him: "Yes, honey?"

Roderick asked me what I was doing, and I told him I was writing in my journal.

Roderick just ran back to the family room, and then I hear Gary ask him, "What did your mom say?"

My head is pounding at this point because Gary won't talk to me. He's using Roderick as a messenger. Here comes another night where nothing will be resolved, and I'll have to cry myself to sleep because he just doesn't get it. It seems like Gary is intentionally trying to taunt me. To bring me to the point where he will have every excuse under the sun to blame everything on me.

In both marriage and singleness, I have never been the type of woman to be insecure. I always knew what a wife's role was and what it meant to be a helpmeet. But Gary makes me feel like I'm not good enough. Whatever I contribute to this house, and whatever I do as a wife and a mother, is never enough for him. Part of me feels like he only married me because I wanted him to. I feel like he will never fight for us.

Chapter 2

Lust Is Blinding

ERICA REMEMBERED HER LIFE after divorcing Derek and before marrying Gary. She longed, as a little girl, to have the fairytale ending. Oh, was she wrong on so many levels! She could only reminisce on the decent relationships she knew would not last. It wasn't true love, it was one of the many stupid mistakes she made in her young adult life, as most of us do when we don't want to listen to anyone. During that time, she had no one to talk to, not even God—or so she thought. Erica was in sin and wondered if she could ever get back to God.

Writing in her journal kept her sane. She filled it with details of her thoughts, expressions, desires, tragedies, etc. Erica often wrote about her past love and wondered how life could have been if they were free to love each other. He already had a woman, and once she knew that, not one moral fiber in her could stay in that relationship. Most of us have our limits and those boundaries we won't cross consciously. We sometimes question how did we got into these messes? Lust was blinding. The possibility that he was the one and not observing the red flags so blatantly visible. How could she not see?

On that December day when she found out he had a wife, and she was the other woman, and she was possibly a home wrecker, she wrote him a goodbye letter. A letter that would make Mother Theresa Proud or at least herself.

Dear Mr. You Know Who,

It isn't often that you find yourself in a situation when you have to make decisions that will affect the rest of your life. If this letter finds you, then I have truly done what is right and not be the other woman who breaks up a marriage. I write this letter to thank you for being someone I could confide in and trust. Although it was a false sense of security, you made me feel safe and wanted. I thought what we had together was special— so special that no one could know about it. Many nights, I called out your name, wishing you were next to me, but that was not reality. I was alone and could not be with you like I wanted. I often wondered why, but fear kept me from asking. I didn't want to lose what we had. Our first and only time together was in February, and it was a day I will never forget.

Since that day, we've had many opportunities to be with each other, but I wondered why it never happened? You would tell me we could not be together because I'd be wrong to cheat on my boyfriend (what a load of crap that was). I would laugh and say you were right, but then something would pull us back to each other. I know now that it was the weakness of our flesh.

One day you'd come in, and we would let everybody know I was your number one. Only God knows why my boyfriend didn't leave me when he said he would. I was very honest when I told you he was talking about leaving, but he never did, and you said he wouldn't (maybe you jinxed it, ha-ha). It was a mistake to think that being with two guys at once was okay. M moral compass was broken.

I truly believe everything happens for a reason, and the time we shared was no exception. I believe you were in my life to show me what I really am—broken. You gave me what he didn't—laughter, normal conversation, and a feeling of sensuality. The enemy is so cunning. The enemy that we so readily allowed to use us like puppets.

On that note, I must realize we do not always get what we want. I have to face the reality that at this point in my life, I will never have the complete package (you). Does anyone ever really find "the complete package" in a mate, or will we all have fleeting fantasies to confront? I don't even know why my boyfriend and I continue in our relationship; it isn't like we are married. I was hoping you and I could be together instead. But we can't, and it isn't only because I have a boyfriend. It is mainly because you are married.

What was I thinking? What were you thinking? We weren't, and that isn't even an excuse. If you weren't afraid to lose your wife, then you would have divorced her by now. But you didn't; you are still hers. Because of this truth, I accept you will never be free to love me.

You accepted me for who I was, but I never knew the real you until now. You encouraged me to be happy and improve myself. I am still working toward becoming a better me, and I hope you will look at yourself and make some changes in your own life. You have a gift of encouraging people, and you gave me what I so desperately needed from a man. Not that I needed your approval or anything, but it felt good to have support from a man, especially since I don't get it at home. But I was wrong to step outside of my relationship to see if the grass was greener on your side.

Though encouraging, I know none of your words were true. Do I believe anything that you have said to me? Absolutely not! You have a hidden agenda, and because of that, I don't know if we can ever be friends.

I do not take friendships lightly, and I guess that is why I have very few genuine friends as it is. You lied to me, and you haven't been honest about anything. You did not tell me you were married. If you had, our relationship would have never gone beyond the boundaries of a friendship. I have too much self-respect to become the other woman, but I unknowingly became just that.

As I close this letter, I do hope we both find what we need. I hope we make the best of who we are and what we have right now. Tomorrow is not promised to us, and I know God will help us out of our mess if we are sincere in doing what right in His sight. The rest of our lives will be what we make of it. I know we still have dreams to fulfill and goals to obtain. You broke my heart, but I will cherish our moment in time as a great lesson learned.

Sincerely,

Ms. You Know Who.

That was the last time Erica contacted him. Although he claimed he understood her feelings and admired her for taking a stand, he was not ready to let her go; he tried to persuade her to stay in his life. Typical, she thought. Because they were in the same undergraduate course, she had to change her schedule and find another class. She took the easy way out, avoidance. Every fiber of her being knew that for her to stand on her morals—or what morals she had left—she would have to remove herself from the situation and move on with her life. Eventually, she got around to breaking up with her boyfriend as well, and that was when she met Gary and fell in love.

It was hard for her to let go of relationships. If it had not been for her fear of being alone, she could probably see how God kept her when she had no one. She had not been on her own since her first husband left. Whenever her relationships ended, she tried her hardest to avoid looking like a failure by finding a new man to fill that void in her life. Despite her feeble attempts, she never took separation very well. She hid her feelings, but she knew she could never hide them from God.

As time passed, she eventually rediscovered her relationship with God because of the mess she had made of her life. She did her first works over, based on the scripture she read in Revelations 2:5, *"Look how far you have fallen! Turn back to me and do the works you did at first. If you don't repent, I will come and remove your lampstand from its place..."* (NLT) She had to look at how far she had fallen. She prayed and read God's word for her life and for her family. Change had to come. Her life had to be better than this.

Erica's journal entry:

I feel sick inside, knowing that I give advice to others using my own words instead of the words God wants me to speak. I am a backslider, and I know that this time around, it will be even harder to get back into a close relationship with Him. I know I have a fight on my hands, but I have to fight in order to be free from misery.

What is God doing with me? What is my life going to be like ten years from now? Will God tell me what He wants me to do? What is my purpose in life? Will I ever know if I am really doing God's will? Will my children grow up to be good men? Will this marriage survive the stress and strains of life? Will I ever find out how to have a relationship with God?

Chapter 3

Fighting Back

DREAMING MORE A LOT LATELY. Some were pleasant and peaceful, and some were so disturbing that she tried to erase them from her memory. In the first dream, she saw an empty schoolyard with no children playing in the field. Bright feathers began to fall like snowflakes, but they would not melt when they landed in her hand. The surrounding air turned gloomy, and the sky looked as if it were about to rain. The feathers swirled and circled around her as if she were in the center of a small tornado. As she looked up at the sky, Erica noticed a bright light coming toward her. She could only see a faint image, but she knew immediately that it was Jesus coming to see and talk to her.

Before Jesus could say anything, she woke up. Lying in bed awake from the dream, she felt a peace she couldn't explain.

In a second dream, this time it was one of the most disturbing dreams she ever had. She did not initially recognize the disguised man as the devil. He seduced her, and together they conceived a child, and gave birth to a daughter. Once Erica realized that the man was really the devil, she could trick him into feeling secure about her loyalty and love for him. Eventually, she rescued her daughter from the devil and fled, but she had to monitor her surroundings constantly. She didn't feel safe anywhere, and felt no peace.

Erica didn't know what these dreams meant and didn't feel comfortable sharing them with anyone. Perhaps they were warnings or confirmations about her future, she thought. When she started seeking God about her relationships, she had more dreams than she could remember. Was God trying to tell her something through these dreams? Erica had no clue, but she firmly believed that God would eventually disclose the significance of these dreams to her. She tried many times to interpret her dreams, but with great frustration, she could never figure them out.

~

Erica was lying down in the bed trying to go to sleep. It was a sultry night in August, and she felt the urge to write. Only the light from the moon beamed through the window to her room. God was giving her ideas and scriptures for her book. Tossing and turning, she shared her thoughts with her husband.

"I think I'm going to write again," Erica said to her Gary, seeking his approval. He remained silent. "Every time I say this to you, you look like you're thinking: 'Oh no, here we go again.'"

"Honey," Gary replied. "It's not that I don't enjoy reading what you write, but you always want me to give you an honest opinion of your work. When I say something, you don't like, you don't speak to me for at least a day or so until you have calmed down. Besides, you end up writing what you want to write, anyway."

She looked at him and smiled. "You are right," she said. "I apologize for that, but you are the only person I trust to read my work."

"Well, this time, don't ask me to read it. I'll read it if you get published, so I can talk about the book if the press asks me questions."

"That right there is why I don't enjoy asking you to read my work. You can be so sarcastic sometimes. Ugh!" Erica threw up her hands in frustration.

Without speaking another word, Gary got up from the bed and walked away from the conflict. He headed straight to the family room to watch television.

Feeling upset and unsettled, Erica tried to fall asleep but couldn't stop tossing and turning. "I can't go to sleep," she kept mumbling. It was becoming harder and harder for Erica to deal with Gary's attitude at home, especially after she expressed to him her desire to write again. In her spare time, and despite her grief and stress, Erica wrote until she had twenty-one pages to claim as her recent work.

Several weeks prior, while standing in the prayer line at church, an intercessor spoke a prophetic word to Erica, which would soon come to pass. The prophecy instructed her to stay silent and allow God to work on her behalf.

She felt led to read I Peter 5:8-9, *"Be alert and of sober mind. Your enemy the devil prowls around like a roaring lion looking for someone to devour. Resist him, standing firm in the faith, because you know that the family of believers throughout the world is undergoing the same kind of sufferings.* (NIV).

God had been preparing Erica for the enemy's attack, but when the attack came, she could do nothing but pray, fast, and call on the Lord for help.

Erica called her friend Yolanda, whom she had not spoken to in weeks. She was surprised to discover that Yolanda had been thinking about her. Yolanda said that God had placed a scripture on her heart for Erica: Psalm 121: 1-8: *"I lift my eyes to the mountains—where does my help come from? My help comes from the Lord, the Maker of heaven and earth. He will not let your foot slip—he who watches over you will not slumber; Indeed, he who watches over Israel will neither slumber nor sleep. The Lord watches over you— the Lord is your shade at your right hand; the sun will not harm you by day, nor the moon by night. The Lord will keep you from all harm—he will watch over your life; the Lord will watch over your coming and going both now and forevermore"* (NIV).

These words encouraged Erica. She believed God heard her cry. Erica had to hold on to see what the end would be. She now believed God would carry her through this valley and keep her safe. He would give her the grace she needed to live according to His Word. There was nothing else for her to do but pray and go through the trial with her husband. No matter how long it took, she knew God would make things good in the end.

As Erica was finding her way back to God, she continued to attend church faithfully. One day, a prophetic word was spoken over the congregation. As the explanation of what was shared went forth, she took it to heart, as if the preacher were speaking to her directly. He spoke about a brand-new life and shared testimonies to show proof of God's goodness. God was giving grace and restoration to His people. The preacher instructed the members to declare God's favor in their lives. Blessings would come easily and would not require hard labor, but there would be some challenges to pass before the blessings would come. There were three requirements for this prophecy to be fulfilled:

1.   Do not allow fear to apprehended you.

The preacher based this on Joshua 1:6-7, 9, *"Be strong and courageous because you will lead these people to inherit the land, I swore to their ancestors to give them. Be strong and very courageous. Be careful to obey all the law my servant Moses gave you; do not turn from it to the right or to the left, that you may be successful wherever you go. Have I not commanded you? Be strong and courageous. Do not be afraid; do not be discouraged, for the Lord your God will be with you wherever you go"* (NIV).

2.   Have faith.

The preacher based this on Hebrews 11:14-19, 32-39, *"People who say such things show that they are looking for a country of their own. If they had been thinking of the country they had left, they would have had the opportunity to return. Instead, they were longing for a better country—a heavenly one. Therefore, God is not ashamed to be called their God, for he has prepared a city for them. By faith, Abraham, when God tested him, offered Isaac as a sacrifice. He who had embraced the promises was about to sacrifice his one and only son, even though God had said to him, 'It is through Isaac that your offspring will be reckoned,' Abraham reasoned that God could even raise the dead, and so in a manner of speaking, he did receive Isaac back from death."*

"And what more shall I say? I do not have time to tell about Gideon, Barak, Samson, and Jephthah, about David and Samuel and the prophets, who through faith conquered kingdoms, administered justice, and gained what was promised; who shut the mouths of the lions, quenched the fury of the flames, and escaped the edge

of the sword; whose weakness was turned to strength; and who became powerful in battle and routed foreign armies. Women received back their dead, raised to life again. There were others who were tortured, refusing to be released so that they might gain an even better resurrection. Some faced jeers and flogging, and even chains and imprisonment. They were put to death by stoning; they were sawed in two; they were killed by the sword. They went about in sheepskins and goatskins, destitute, persecuted, and mistreated—the world was not worthy of them. They wandered in deserts and mountains, living in caves and in holes in the ground. These were all commended for their faith, yet none of them received what had been promised, since God had planned something better for us so that only together with us would they be made perfect" (NIV).

3. Stay strong.

Weakness sets up a person for depression. When people are depressed, they can't move forward in God. The preacher based this requirement on Isaiah 41:10 and Exodus 15:2.

Isaiah 41:10: *"So do not fear, for I am with you, do not be dismayed, for I am your God. I will strengthen you and help you; I will uphold you with my righteous right hand"* (NIV).

Exodus 15:2: *"The Lord is my strength and my defense; He has become my salvation. He is my God, and I will praise Him, my father's God, and I will exalt Him"* (NIV).

Chapter 4

Dreaming Again

LIFE CONTINUED TO GET WORSE as the marriage got even more strange. Erica had another dream. This time it was short but vivid.

She recorded this dream in her journal:

The world was looking like the last days, as described in the Bible. Everything was chaotic. The rapture had not yet taken place because I was still there. My family members were still alive as well (those I knew for sure were going to heaven). It appears I was in charge of some type of rebel offense or military operation, which I could not distinguish in the dream. There were seven people who would be key players in the battles to come. I was in command to print out the names of seven people. I only remember one name: Michael Being.

Erica couldn't decide if her dreams had meaning. 'Maybe she dreamed this because she watched a movie', she thought. Maybe it's because the soldiers in Iraq were still being killed for no good reason. But what if God was trying to tell her something? The dream was frustrating, to say the least.

Trusting God was hard, but she continued to believe that her life was safe in His hands. Before going to work, she would pray in the mornings for twenty or thirty minutes, and then she would read her Bible in the office before her day started. It was the only routine she could keep, but as for her life itself, she felt like she was being pulled in ten different directions. She had church, her work, her children and their sports, her husband, and, on top of all that, the next semester of classes was about to start. After Erica completed her bachelor's degree, Norwich University accepted her into their graduate program. She was pursuing a degree in justice administration and criminology through the two-year program. Where would this program lead her? Was this a dead end? Did she seek God long enough to hear His answer about going back to school?

~

One day, after a major argument with her husband, Erica had gone to bed and dreamed termites were eating the wood underneath her house. She was standing outside with four other people whom she did not recognize because their faces were blurred. They stood outside talking about the termites eating away at the foundation of the house.

The dreamed switched to Erica trying to get medical insurance for her daughter. After filling out packets so her daughter could see a doctor, as they stood in line, Erica saw people disappear—instantly she realized it was the rapture. For a split second, she doubted her salvation and felt terrified of what was to come, but then she felt herself transform. As she held her daughter's hand, she floated. She felt jubilation in her spirit because she had escaped being left behind to go through the tribulation period.

Waking up from the dream, Erica felt like the termites might have been a reference to her marriage. Something was eating away at it, and only God could exterminate the problem. Erica worried about her future with Gary. Her only solace was found in believing that God would prepare her for whatever was to come. The dream about her daughter confused her because Erica only had sons.

Reality hit Erica as she got up from the bed. Her son Greg's birthday party was today. He was turning ten.

"Honey, wake up," Erica said to Gary. "We have to get ready for Greg's party."

Gary was quiet a moment before answering. "I have been up for two hours already. You woke me up as you were talking in your sleep. What were you dreaming about? You just kept repeating: 'Please God, do not leave me here.'" Gary agitated.

She looked at him and pondered whether she should even tell him. "I dreamed about the rapture."

Erica started explaining her dream to Gary, but before she could finish, "I don't want to hear about it." He left the room. Erica sat on her side of the bed and realized planning her son Greg's tenth birthday party had been a joy. This would be his first big birthday party just for him. Erica had prepared everything herself and had not expected Gary to help with anything other than cooking some of the food. But the tension still grew. Erica knew Gary would get neurotic because she was not doing things the way he thought she should do them.

Erica made the invitations herself, which saved her a bit of money. Praying for the past two days, she had made it clear this party was for Greg. Gary would often turn the party's into something for himself, then his sons. Erica didn't mind that he liked to entertain guests, but she wanted the party centered on the kids. As trivial as it seemed, Gary was adamant about playing his adult contemporary music. She was relieved that she had bought children's music, which she played to drown out what Gary was playing inside the house.

As they prepared for the day, Erica and the boys continued setting everything up, and there had been no arguing because Gary left and didn't come back for a couple of hours. She wondered why he did not tell her where he was going and also why he left when he was supposed to help with the party. Eventually, Gary came back but brought an attitude with him. Erica prayed the party would run smoothly despite his attitude. As Greg's party was underway, Erica played children's music without a peep from Gary. The party was a success.

The next day, Gary rose to greet his sons with the affection of a loving father. And then, he greeted Erica with a pat on the head and said, "How is everything going?" In the eleven years that they had been together, Gary never patted Erica on the head. She didn't know what to make of it, but she didn't jump to any conclusions. It was true that they had not made love in quite some time. Sickness and busyness had gotten in the way. A week of no intimacy turned into 6 months, and then a year had passed. Erica welcomed the break, during the first week, but she no longer felt secure in their marriage. She approached him several times about it, but he never gave an answer as to why they were no longer intimate. She had no proof that Gary was cheating on her, though she suspected it. Still, she was careful not to accuse him without having proof.

~

Erica would often sit alone in her car on mornings after she dropped off the boys to school. She would sit and listen to 107.9 KWAVE, a Christian radio station. This morning, the topic was on sexual immorality. The minister preached about how sex was not meant to occur outside of marriage. Like many women, Erica had sex before marriage. She eventually married two out of the four men she had premarital sex with, but still she knew she had given up her body too soon. Her first marriage failed, and she was afraid that this one would fail too.

Erica prayed and then remembered things that happened in her childhood. At a young age, Erica had been in sexual encounters with boys. It started in the fifth grade when she had a boyfriend who lived across the street from the elementary school she attended. This boy and his friend were Erica's schoolmates, and she also had a friend named Christine. They would all hang out together; adults were rarely home to supervise them. Although no sex took place, they explored each other's bodies.

Several years later, it came to light that Erica's childhood friend, Christine, had endured molestation and rape by her stepfather throughout elementary school. She eventually became a prostitute because of what happened to her, which started in the third grade.

Erica had a vague recollection of a neighborhood boy, five years older than her, almost molesting her. Erica quickly removed herself from the situation and never told a soul. She did not have another sexual encounter until she met her first husband, Derek. She had not remembered this part of her childhood until now and realized that these experiences may have been the root of her struggle with fornication. Finally discovering her bondage, she could release it to God.

Erica continued to pray for her marriage, but it wasn't getting any better. She prayed God would work a miracle in Gary's life. As much as Gary claimed to know God, he didn't act like it. He followed his own way.

The more she prayed, the more they argued. Gary flatly refused counseling—especially Christian counseling. He accused Erica of trying to force her beliefs on him. Despite the temptation to cuss him out, she refrained from doing so, understanding that it wouldn't solve anything. There has to be a way to reason with him somehow. 'Maybe I can communicate my true feelings and thoughts about our marriage to him through a letter, hoping he will read it and recognize the potential for positive changes. Maybe he would see I was trying to save our marriage and meet me halfway to resolve the issues between us. I never threatened to leave him. He'll see that I've been trying to make things work between us,' she thought.

Erica wrote the letter to Gary and gave it to him inside a Father's Day card. She didn't know how he would react to it or even if he would read it. Considering the way, he is acted toward her lately, she wouldn't be surprised if he decided to walk out the door for good, just like Derrick did.

This letter was something she felt she had to write him. Erica continued to pray that God would save Gary. She so desperately wanted peace in her life that she was prepared to face Gary, even if her confrontation made him decide to walk out the door on his own terms. Although she knew God could save him, she started to give up on the marriage. She didn't feel like this was a marriage anymore; it felt like two roommates who couldn't stand each other.

Their relationship was a rollercoaster ride from hell.

One minute, Gary would love her, and then his anger would erupt when she did something he didn't like. She thought back to the time they started dating until now. Nothing Gary had ever done wrong caused her to feel as turned off and disgusted as she felt now. During one of their arguments, he said, "F*** Jesus." This was the first time he ever referenced her faith and beliefs in a derogatory manner. Erica thought, 'If I didn't have Christ in my life, I know he wouldn't have said it. It was intended to hurt me a great deal. My warfare is not carnal but spiritual.

Erica did not want to lose her salvation over any man. God had brought her this far with Gary; He could change his heart. God did not want any of his children to perish, but she wondered if Gary's heart was so hardened that God would turn him over to a reprobate. What if he decided to stay married but still refused to change his ways? What if Erica was stuck with no peace for the rest of their marriage?

Gary had read the letter, and although it was laced with apologies and realness, he didn't take to heart any of the words Erica wrote.

~

The next morning, Erica was up washing her car. Gary appeared in front of the house with flowers and a card. With all arrogance and pride, he said, "An apology is an open door for you to continue in the same behavior you are apologizing for. Change the behavior, or no one else will care. Sarcasm will get you nowhere, and counseling won't help either. You need to change the behavior."

This was classic signs of Narcissistic behavior. He had an inflated sense of self-importance. There was no accountability on his part. Everything was directed at Erica, as to why things were as bad as they were in their marriage. He was ignoring the needs of his wife and children.

Gary had said so many times that eventually Erica was going to hate him. At that point in their marriage, she was doing just that. She cried out to God to do something: "God, please let him leave us. Put it in his mind to just walk out. I can't take this anymore!"

After an hour of complaining, she felt an urge to search the scriptures. The first scripture she read was Psalm 102:1–4, *"Hear my prayer, Lord; let my cry for help come to you. Do not hide your face from me when*

I am in distress. Turn your ear to me; when I call, answer me quickly. For my days vanish like smoke; my bones burn like glowing embers. My heart is blighted and withered like grass; I forget to eat my food." (NIV) This scripture strengthened Erica, as well as Psalm 27:1–14 and Psalm 28. They encouraged her to hold on to God's unchanging hand.

For a while, Erica and Gary did not speak to each other. Their conversations were brief. All Erica could do was think about how she wanted to tell him he was a mean bastard, but keeping that to herself was best. 'Lord, forgive me for what I'm thinking,' she thought.

The whole time they had been together, she always supported him no matter what he did, but it was never enough for him. His words continued to hurt her, and he didn't seem to care that they hurt. If God didn't change him, Erica knew he would never change. The only hope for their marriage was salvation for Gary. Gary would mumble negative comments about Erica, saying that she was lazy, but he avoided addressing her directly. She figured he was probably going through the mid-life change. He was fifty-three years old and could be feeling inadequate, or maybe looking for an excuse to get out of their marriage. Time and time again, she wanted to ask him to leave, but she was afraid it would provoke him to hurt her more with his words. She wanted him to leave on his own like her first husband did.

Over the years, Gary hinted to Erica many times that he wanted to leave her. He would ask Erica if she wanted him to go. She never responded, and he never left. He had to be just as miserable as she was or, as the idiom goes—misery loves company.

~

Erica was attracted to the inner person, but by the time they decided to show their true colors, it was always too late in the relationship. She met Darin after the split from her first marriage. He was six feet six inches tall, muscular, and twenty-seven-years-young. He was also a former Colorado Panther Football player who still lived with his mother. Darin had not made it to the pros, but his college degree qualified him to teach athletics. Darin and Erica had been talking over the phone before they met, and when they finally met for the first time, she had to pick him up for the date because he didn't have a car. She should have recognized that something was wrong, but she thought Darin wouldn't last long anyway and figured she would enjoy the fling while it lasted. Contrary to her plan, Erica's relationship with Darin grew, and she gave him her body because her flesh was in need. She felt like she couldn't function without a man's touch. Turns out, she was taking Darin to work three times a week, and most of the time she would buy him lunch and paid for their dates. Desperate to be married again, she wanted to have a family with someone. With whom, she didn't care. She finally came to her senses and broke it off with Darin, only to find herself entangled in a love affair with Johnston, whom she later found out was a married man. Of course, things didn't go right with Johnston either, so she swore to herself that she would never get involved with another man unless he was a man of faith.

A year later, she started dating Gary, after knowing him for five years prior. He had become her best friend—someone she could talk to about anything. He believed in God. It was rare to find a good man who was intelligent, with a car, and a degree to back it all up. Gary was the shoulder she could cry on. He would encourage her so much that she felt like she could take on the world. He was a military, fun loving guy. He wanted what she wanted. Erica fell deeply in love with him. Gary was Erica's knight in shining armor, and because they were friends first, she thought he was the 'one'. But she never sought God about him. She made up in her own mind that he was the person she should spend the rest of her life with. Even during his three-year stint in the Army Reserve in Kuwait, she wouldn't look at another man. She would hear songs and imagine he was singing them to her or she would sing them to him. They wrote each other letters every week and sent photos of each other.

Gary had a three-day leave, and before going back to finish his six months, he asked Erica to marry him. Doubt was in the back of her mind because she didn't know if he truly wanted to get married. She thought maybe he was just trying to please her. At least back then, he considered her feelings and desires in life. Even with the doubt, she didn't hesitate to say yes to his proposal. Looking back on things now, she realized she didn't get to know Gary or any of the men she had dated. They kept skeletons in their closets. Erica didn't realize Gary's true colors until they were five years into the marriage.

Gary expressed to Erica that counseling would not help her, but she thought better of the idea and went anyway. She hated him for a brief while, but she also recognized that her choices were the reason she was in this position in the first place, and she had to allow God to fight this battle for her. She had to continue to believe that God would change in Gary's life and soften his heart so that he could receive true salvation through Christ Jesus, the Son of the living God.

Erica continued to pray her marriage would not be in vain and that God would help them grow stronger as a union. She vowed to herself that if this marriage failed, she would never marry again and would make God her husband because she was tired of making the same mistakes. She didn't want to go through the pain of enduring an unhealthy relationship again, and she didn't want her children to experience that pain either.

It appeared the men she married had no sincerity or willingness to compromise or work out their differences of opinions. The men she loved were strong, but they had no compassion. For them, it was all or nothing, and she couldn't understand why. She felt as though they always tried to take the straightforward way out, or they would make demands with such high expectations that when their expectations weren't met, they would use that as an excuse to leave.

Every man she had been with expected her to change who she was and compromise her standards. She had to suffer the consequences of marrying men who had not truly given their lives to God. Men who claimed to be something they were not.

Erica often imagined how it would be if Gary truly gave his life to God. She knew arguments were a part of all relationships, but she believed her marriage would have fewer problems if Gary were saved. As of right now, she felt like she was living in hell. Jesus has the key; I'm just waiting for Him to let me out of this prison, she thought. Erica was miserable and knew she had to seek the Lord in order to maintain her sanity.

It was Father's Day again, and Erica took Gary to the Queen Mary for a surprise dinner. They were barely speaking to each other, so it was a silent drive. The host seated them at a secluded booth. Gary allowed Erica to order first, and it wasn't long before he started with his typical negative comments. She thought at least this day, he would be on his best behavior. Unfortunately, he says, "You really don't get it, do you? What you ordered does not impress me. Make sure you're eating healthily when you're not around me."

Her expectation for a good evening was shattered. Her first mind was to cancel the reservations but knew she would never hear the end of it if she hadn't planned something for him. After having two children, Erica had picked up a little weight, and Gary took every opportunity to remind her he did not like the way she looked. Erica held back her emotions, but tears fell from her eyes, reflecting her deep hurt and disappointment. She silently waited for her food to come, and when it came, she took a couple of bites and could not eat anymore. Gary had ruined her appetite. Erica hadn't eaten all day because she was busy helping the boys pick out gifts for their dad. She finished her water, walked to the cashier, paid for their meals, and left Gary in the restaurant. She had it in her mind to leave him there, but she would not stoop to his level. So, she waited in the car for him to come out. When he finally did, she took him straight home.

The minute he got out of the car, Erica drove off, and her screeching tires were more than enough of a statement. Once again, Erica was furious, frustrated, and hurt by Gary's words. Why did she even bother to take him to dinner in the first place? Why would a person choose a restaurant to put someone on blast like he did to her? Why did he feel the need to think that what she ordered was to impress him? It was his arrogance that bothered her the most.

When Erica arrived home five hours later, she went straight to the room where he was watching television and confronted him about the dinner. "Is your egomaniac, self-centered, self-seeking thoughts so twisted you would think that I was trying to impress you with my order? Where is your mind? Why do you think your opinion is that important to me? You have no consideration for anyone else but yourself. You are so selfish, and I am ashamed to even be married to you right now!"

All Erica ever wanted from Gary was his love and support, and although she might have had a part of his heart, she never received support or communication from him to help solve any of their problems. Gary never said a word, so she turned and walked out of the room. She could only depend on her faith and strength in God. Her hope of having a loving, cohesive marriage was in the hands of the Lord; she casted all her cares upon Him.

Erica isolated herself and only wanted people around her who would give her encouragement to make it through. Not that she didn't appreciate Gary's candid nature. She realized the enemy was mean and brutal.

Gary's words were always mean-spirited, and he often recognized his own traits, but he did nothing to change them. He believed it was okay to talk to people the way he did, and Erica never had the nerve to ask him why he thought it was okay. Erica had failed God many times in being too confrontational, but this time there was nothing holding her back, and she felt comfortable to say what she needed to say to Gary.

After that night, Gary started sleeping in the guest room and coming home even later than usual. Recognizing the signs, Erica asked him one last time to go to marriage counseling, but he flat-out refused. He couldn't stand to be in the same room with Erica, even to watch television. It would soon be seven months since he touched her physically.

Chapter 5

At the End of the Rope

ERICA HELD ONTO GOD to keep her spiritually and physically. She still yearned for Gary's touch, but she did not pursue a physical relationship, and neither did he. She prayed daily that God would keep her from temptation. The enemy knew that sexual immorality was what she had struggled with since the age of eleven, so it wasn't long before the test came again when Johnston Matthews saw her alone in the coffee shop on Wilton Place. "Erica is that you?" She turned around to see the face of a familiar voice. "Wow, Johnston, is that you? It is so nice to see you! How have you been?" They embraced each other with a hug.

"Erica, I am a blessed man of God. I am doing great. Do you have a minute to talk?"

"Yes, I have time."

"I just wanted you to know that God has answered my prayer. I have been praying for a chance to reunite with you for about a year now. Please, sit down." Johnston gestured toward the seats behind him. They both sat at a table next to the window. "Well, after you broke up with me, I found out that I had cancer."

"Oh no! How are you doing now?"

"Well, once I found out I had cancer, I told my wife, and she said I had it coming for all the cheating I had done."

"You mean to tell me I was not the only one?" Her hands hiding her mouth.

"Unfortunately, I was stupid several times. You weren't the first, but you were the last. Anyway, to make a long story short, she divorced me because she thought I was going to die. After the divorce, I went through the chemotherapy alone and found myself seeking God again. I did a one-eighty back toward serving the Lord. During chemo, I rededicated my life and have never looked back. Now, I am an ordained elder and assistant pastor at New Bethany Church in Long Beach and cancer free."

"Oh, my goodness! That is insane."

In an instant, Johnston thought about the life he could've had with Erica had they never broken up.

"So, tell me how you've been, Erica."

"Where do I begin? After I finished school, I started working in mid- Wilshire, and I got married to my current husband, Gary. We were head-over-heels in love and now, eleven years later, our marriage is falling apart. Unfortunately, once again, I was disobedient to the will of God concerning marriage and married a man that was not saved and had not truly sold out to God. We have two sons together, and you remember Nolan, don't you?"

"Yes, I do. How is he doing?"

"He's doing great. He's excelling in school and sports. My other two boys are doing great as well. I pray fervently that God will restore my marriage, but I know that it is in God's timing and not mine. After I got married, I too rededicated my life to the Lord and truly sought God for what He wanted to do with my life. I started writing again, and I am almost finished with my third novel."

"Did you ever publish your first novel?" Shocked that he even remembered.

"As a matter of fact, I did. Since you asked, I'm guessing you haven't read it. I just so happen to have a copy with me. I'll autograph it for you."

"Thank you so much. I will definitely read it and tell you what I think."

"Johnston, if nothing else, I could always count on you to be honest about my writing. If I ask my husband to read it and help me out, he always comes up with some excuse as to why he can't." Erica sipped her mocha latte and thought better about the conversation and what she was spilling to a man she once knew intimately.

"Erica, I know things can't be that bad."

"Johnston, if it weren't for God keeping me peaceful and not allowing my mind to wander, I would definitely believe that my husband is cheating on me. But I don't have proof, and I'm not going to waste my time looking for any. I know the enemy will try to plant a seed, but I also know that if it is happening, God will reveal it just like he did in my last marriage. I feel that at this point, we are two ships passing in the night. It will be up to God to restore our marriage or put it asunder. You of all people know I think marriage is sacred, and I won't be the one to tell him to leave. I mean, at this point, we hardly ever speak to each other anyway. He will have to tell me himself. In the meantime, I have to keep living and taking care of the boys like God wants me to live. Through all my tests and trials, God has made me strong. To be honest, I was devastated when I walked away from our relationship. It tore me up inside that I didn't know how wrong we were in the beginning. Once I knew the truth, I really had no other choice but to walk away. This time, the difference is I can't simply walk away from my marriage because I know God wouldn't honor that. I've asked Gary to go to marriage counseling, but he refused. He asked me to forgive him for his infidelity the first time, but now I can't tell if he's cheating on me again. There is nothing I can do now other than pray and wait on the Lord for the change to come."

Johnston smiled at Erica, and she was surprised at his reaction. "It is truly amazing how you've grown in the Lord." They sat there in silence for ten seconds sipping on their coffee. Erica looked out the smoke-colored windows as the traffic went by.

"Erica, if you ever want to talk, here's my number at home and at the church. Use those numbers if you want to."

"Johnston, I've talked to you too much already, but it was never hard to talk to you, was it? We used to talk for hours and hours at a time, and we would always have something good to say about each other. That was before I found out you were married."

"You are right. I was desperate to have the kind of marriage my parents had, and I didn't care about how I got it. What I didn't realize until later was that they loved God first, and God took care of their love for each other. I mean, through my whole ordeal, I thought my wife would stick with me through thick and thin. For the most part, she did, but when I could no longer provide her with the financial lifestyle she was accustomed to, she showed that she had not forgiven me for my adultery or for getting sick for that matter. I even asked her if she wanted me to leave and divorce her, and she said no and that she had forgiven me.

"We went to marriage counseling, and I asked her for forgiveness in front of our therapist. Even after we divorced and I started living the life God wanted me to live, I asked her to forgive me again. If I hadn't done that and had not been truly seeking God for my deliverance, I probably would have been devastated at the fact that she wouldn't take me back. I had done everything God required me to do, and when she turned me down again, I felt okay with it. I was released from our marriage covenant. She has since remarried, and you know the devil is always busy seeking whom he may devour. She has tried to get back with me, but I know that it is only because God has restored my health and has blessed me to be where I am now.

"While I am at it, I want to truly apologize to you and ask you for forgiveness. I am sorry for lying to you and taking advantage of your feelings for me. I never meant to hurt you that way. I truly thought that it would be nothing more than a one-night stand and that it wouldn't go any further, but it did. I dragged you into my mess, and for that, I am truly sorry."

"Mr. Johnston Matthews, you are truly forgiven, but I too must take the blame for my actions. I did not have to give in to your advances. I chose to sin with you. The only forgiveness needed is from God."

Erica stood up to get ready to leave. She hugged Johnston and thanked him for listening.

"I'll give you a call, plus, I need to bring you my other book."

"No bother, I have them both. But you can stop by and sign my other copy."

"Ah! You did read my books! I will come and visit your church when you preach. I will talk to you later. I have to get back to work."

"I will be speaking next Sunday. If you get a chance, come by."

"I definitely will." She turned and walked out the door. Erica felt giddy inside. She felt that spark she had always experienced when she had feelings for someone of the opposite sex. As soon as she walked out of the café doors, she went into prayer. Johnston's persona was what she had longed for in a husband.

~

She prayed and fasted for three days before she went to visit Johnston's church. The church was a fifteen-mile drive from her home. She was able to leave the boys at home and visit by herself. She was uncomfortable at first but felt at ease after praying. Erica had on a teal-and-black ensemble with the purse and shoes to match.

She arrived at church before the service started to make sure she got a good seat. Erica asked the usher where Johnston might be. "He is in his office preparing to give the message. May I tell him who is asking for him?" Erica felt like the usher's tone was sarcastic. "No, thank you dear. I'm trying to surprise him. I'll just see him after the service. Thank you." The woman walked toward another usher who was a short distance from where Erica was sitting. "She wouldn't even give me her name," Erica heard the woman say. Both ushers stared at her all service long.

As Johnston went up to preach the message, Erica's mind wondered why she was there. Why was she at this church, and why did she encounter Johnston again? 'Run girl, run, she reasoned to herself.' The battle raged as she sat quietly in the seat. 'Run out of this church as fast as you can. You know what's going to happen if you stay…No…The devil is a lie, and the truth is not in him. I am going to stay and hear the Word.' Boy! Was the devil busy. As she sat there listening to Johnston, it was as if he were speaking directly to her. 'God works that way, doesn't he?' She thought. She felt encouraged to hold on to her marriage. Once again, God used Johnston to encourage Erica. As he finished the altar call, he stood to recognize the visitors in the church. Erica felt like sneaking out, but she knew that she would be too obvious.

"I would also like to thank a special and dear friend of mine for coming out to visit us this morning. She has been a great inspiration to me, and she doesn't even know it. Erica, please stand and have words."

Normally, Erica was never lost for words. But this time she was, and she felt like it was best to hold back a little.

"I would like to thank God for being in the house of the Lord this morning. I have known Johnston for quite some time now, and this is the first time I have had a chance to hear him speak God's word so passionately. I greet you from Brighton Community Church, where Thaddeus Hill is my pastor."

'Thank you, Erica. Just to let you all know, she is a well-known author and has two books under her belt. Currently, she's working on her third. I invite you all to read them. They will encourage your soul."

As he relinquished the microphone to the senior pastor, she could hear some women in the back say things like, "I thought I recognized her. I read her books, and they are not all that."

Erica giggled as she realized there had been more than one eye on Elder Matthews.

After service, Erica walked out of the church and waited for Johnston to come out.

"Hey Erica, it is so wonderful to see you again. I am so glad you came. How did you like the sermon?"

"Well, the Word of God is always good. God is truly using you. The anointing of the Holy Spirit was all over you. You spoke to my soul and encouraged me to hold on. I appreciate the change in you. Your spirit has changed, and I felt the sincerity in what you were preaching. Now, on another subject, if I didn't know any better, I would think you had a fan club."

"God gets all the glory. Please excuse the fan club. Some of the women here are not trying to wait on God to bring them a mate. Anyway, my parents are here, and they wanted me to invite you to have dinner with us. Will you come?"

She did not hesitate to answer. "Sure, I'll come. Just let me call home."

"Give me a few minutes to get my parents in the car."

"Okay, but don't leave me because I will follow you." Erica called home, and Nolan answered the phone. "Hey honey. How is everything?"

"Fine, Mom. How was service?"

"It was wonderful. Is Gary home?"

"Yes, he is. Hold on." She waited several seconds for Gary to come to the phone.

"Yeah, what can I do for you?"

Erica looked at the phone. "Hi Gary. I was calling to let you and the boys know that I will be going to dinner with Johnston and his parents."

"Erica, I don't care what you do or where you go. The boys are old enough to take care of themselves, and if they want to eat, then they will fix themselves something to eat. So, I'll see you when I see you."

The heartache set in and the knots formed in the pit of Erica's stomach. The thought of turning down the invitation to dinner crossed her mind, but she worried that Johnston would ask her why the change. Johnston blew at her to signal he was ready. As she drove out the parking lot, she could see the fan club pointing at her.

~

The conversation at the Matthews' residence was light and peaceful. They talked about church and also about happiness and living a fun life. They asked some questions about Erica's children, but no other personal matters were discussed. Erica thought to herself that this was an ideal family to belong to, but she figured that a family couldn't be this perfect. They laughed so much that it hurt, and it seemed so genuine and loving.

"Coffee, anyone?" The question rang from Johnston's lips like a timed alarm clock. His parents declined and wanted to rest in their family room. Erica accepted the offer for coffee, and they both took their coffee outside on the front porch. Johnston looked at Erica as she stared into space. "I'll give you a penny for your thoughts," he said.

Erica thought out her response carefully. "As much as you and I used to have talks, you'd think I could talk to you now," she said. "But I can't even find the words."

"You know I wouldn't pressure you. You know God is with you and you can take everything to Him. I am here unconditionally to listen if you want to talk."

"Do you remember when we used to talk for hours at a time, even after we would have an argument about an article in the paper or something we saw on the news? We could just communicate so well. I remember I did most of the fussing, and you would just look at me like something was wrong with me. When I stopped fussing, you would just smile and stay quiet. I often wondered if you were just waiting for that special moment to tell me about myself, but you never did."

"Nothing about my tactics has changed since then," Johnston said. "I speak when it is necessary. I stay quiet now as much as I did then. You have to pick your battles you know"

"Well, I have to pray much more to do so, but I am quieter than I used to be. Why bother fueling the fire when the other person is not ready to listen? Most of the time, I find myself having no conversation at all with my husband. How can you truly listen to what someone has to say when you think you're always right, and when you don't care about what the other person is saying? Don't take this out of context, but to think I am here with you while my marriage is falling apart. I'm not saying that this is a sin, but what does it mean when I would rather be here with you than at home with my husband? I am truly questioning why I am here? Why did we run into each other at the coffee shop? I know you said you had been praying to see me, but I am so hurt and confused right now. I don't know whether I'm coming or going half of the time. I stay on my knees and pray for God to help me understand this whole situation. How I got myself into another mess of a marriage? I have asked God to show me myself. I have been forced to learn a lot about me, but there is this haunting feeling that nothing is going to change. I feel like it's either God testing me so I will stay prepared, or it's the enemy trying to make me doubt God."

Ten seconds of silence passed. "Erica, I don't even know what to say. I want to hug you so much right now and show you that you can have happiness, but I know it would be inappropriate. I would never do anything against God's will or your marriage."

"The funny part about all of this is that I wouldn't either. I have no desire to be with anyone else. My desire is for my husband to get saved. In any case, I would probably slap you silly and never see you again if you tried something with me." Erica walked over to give Johnston a pat on the shoulder. "I know in your heart that it's not your intention to sin, but we have to be aware of the enemy. I know that the devil is using some of those women at your church mightily." They both laughed and broke the tension in the air that neither one of them knew how to get out of.

"Would you like your coffee refreshed?" Johnston asked.

"Sure," she said after finishing her cup.

As Erica waited for her coffee, she had these thoughts:
'I am still in love with Gary, but I hate him at the same time. I love the person he used to be, but I hate the sin in him now. I want to connect with him physically and emotionally but most of all spiritually these days. I've been feeling less love for him that each day goes by, and I find myself wanting only God and my children in my life. Emotionally, I think I would be ready to forgive his infidelity, if only he was truly repentant and sorry for what he had done. Spiritually, I know God would take away my hurt and pain. Mentally, I am tough and would only cry when necessary. It's the thought of his infidelity that sends fear and mistrust through my veins, sticking its jagged edges deeper in every move. It wasn't that I couldn't allow him to touch me, but every time we did make love after the last affair, I felt a tiny piece of my heart chip away. I couldn't stop thinking about what the other woman did that I failed to do. Gary tried to dispel the notion that the other woman did something to attract him sexually, but his voice that God often allowed me to discern wasn't always truthful, and Gary was never willing to discuss his infidelity.'

As Johnston turned to walk into the house, the ceramic coffee cup Erica was holding shattered and flew everywhere. Johnston tried to revive her but was unsuccessful, so he called 911. Her body lay limp and frozen, but she was breathing.

~

As the ambulance drove her to the National Hospital, Johnston prayed and prayed until Erica slowly opened her eyes in the hospital room. Her mind told her to speak, but nothing was coming out that any human being could understand. When her eyes focused clearly, she was able to distinguish the handsome figure sitting beside her bed. Johnston had not left her side. As her vital signs stabilized, Erica cleared her throat enough to be able to whisper a question. "What happened?"

His face comforted her as he began to explain. "You fainted while you were at my parents' house. The doctors have been running some tests to rule things out. The good news is that you're not pregnant. They called your family and said that they'll be here shortly. The bad news is that you're going to be in here for a while because they want to run more tests."

It was hard for her to talk, but she persevered to get as many questions out as she could. "How long have I been out?"

He adjusted her pillow. "For about two hours. They made sure that you were stable before they moved you out of the emergency room. The doctor asked me to notify him once you were awake, so I'll be right back. I have to let them know."

Erica laughed because Johnston's voice was confident but it didn't match his nervous facial expressions. By the time he returned to the room, her bedside was filled with her family who cared for her and loved her a great deal. Her sons were by her side, hugging and kissing her and asking her questions she could not answer. As Johnston looked at Erica, he could see that she was feeling overwhelmed and needed to be rescued. He stepped right in to relieve the boys of their panic and shock. As the boys tried to hold in their anxiety, they sat in the chairs next to their mother's bed and waited for the doctor to come in.

Johnston introduced himself, and the boys remained calm. They felt comfortable with him being there, even though they knew nothing about him or the past relationship he had with their mother. Nolan was the calmest of the three boys. He caressed Erica's hand as if he were the head of the household, and in many ways, that's what he had become. Their father, Gary, stayed in the waiting area of the hospital, seemingly uninterested.

When the doctor came in, he thought Johnston was Erica's husband, and Nolan politely said, "No sir. I will go and get my dad." No one could understand why Gary acted this way. Five minutes later, Gary came into the room. As the doctor began to talk about the tests they would run on Erica, Johnston tried to excuse himself out of the room to give the family their privacy, but Nolan asked him to stay. Nolan felt an instant connection with Johnston, a connection he never felt with his father. Nolan sensed a genuine kindness from him and wanted to know more about who he was. By this time, Johnston had to leave to check on his own parents; he left his business card with Nolan so that they could update him on Erica's progress.

"Nolan, please make sure you call me tomorrow to let me know how your mother is doing. Let her know that I will try and get back to see her before visiting hours are over."

Nolan stuck out his hand. "Okay, I will let her know. Thank you for being there and praying for my mother."

Nolan loved his mother more than she knew. Withdrawn most of the time in his own world, he was more mature than other boys his age. He loved his stepfather also, but he wasn't dumb or naïve. Sensing that their marriage was tearing his mother apart, he could only speculate at this point in time that this had something to do with his mother's illness. Now that Nolan was seventeen, he was independent and able to take care of himself, but he always kept a respect for his stepfather no matter what.

"Mr. and Mrs. Manning, the tests that we have run so far have shown that you don't have any heart problems. We will keep you and run more tests in the morning. We will conduct an MRI and a CAT scan to determine whether it is neurological in origin, since you have told us you have been having migraine headaches lately. Although we will run tests in the morning, we won't have the results until Tuesday. Right now, you're stable, but we won't know the details until we receive the test results back. I recommend for all of you to go home and get some rest, as Mrs. Manning needs her rest."

As Dr. Hubbard walked out of the room, Gary followed behind. "Doctor, what are your speculations about my wife?"

Dr. Hubbard studied Mr. Manning. To him, Gary didn't show the affection toward his wife that husbands normally had, but he answered his questions. "Mr. Manning, right now, I don't want to speculate because it could be something or it could be nothing at all. The worst-case scenario is that something could be seriously wrong with your wife; the best case is that she's just stressed out and needs rest. Again, I don't want to speculate anything right now. The tests will reveal the truth. The bottom line in all of this is that we have to get to the root of why she fainted. Go home, Mr. Manning, and get some rest. We'll know one way or another by Tuesday morning."

In that short period of uncertainty, Erica prepared herself for whatever God had planned for her life. She had no regrets and was ready for her life to end this way. Erica was a joint heir with Christ and had heaven to look forward to. She loved her children dearly and did not want to leave them behind, but if given the choice, she would welcome seeing Jesus face to face. Erica had a lot of questions to ask Him.

For the first time, Gary felt lost. Erica was the glue that kept them respecting each other. Gary knew that if Erica died, he would have to take responsibility of the boys and everything they had accumulated together, which scared him the most. He was quiet and more withdrawn than before.

As Erica went through the tests, Johnston stayed by her side. Nolan and Johnston traded shifts to watch Erica after the tests were completed.

It was Tuesday, and the results weren't going to be ready until the late morning. Dr. Hubbard told Johnston to call Erica's family so the results could be discussed with everyone. This time, Erica's parents were a part of the ensemble. Everyone gathered, and Erica felt even more at peace now that her mother was by her side.

"I'm so glad you're here."

"I know, honey. We took the flight out last night. If it weren't for Nolan and Johnston, we wouldn't have known what was going on." Her mother's disgust for Gary was evident by her tone.

At this point, Erica still loved Gary, but she felt sorrow for him more than anything else. Her wish through all of this was that Gary would accept Christ as his Lord and Savior. She wanted him to realize that he couldn't live his life without God. He needed help. Erica was willing to go through anything that would plant a seed in Gary's heart to steer him toward salvation. She prayed daily for his salvation, and she knew that God would make a way, but Gary had to be wiling and open to accept God's offer.

Dr. Hubbard walked in the room. It was silent. "We have the results and have determined that it is a tumor." He placed the X-ray sheet on the whiteboard on the wall and turned on the lamp. "If you look at the X-ray here on the white board, the tumor is called Craniopharyngioma. In other words, there is a sac that is producing calcium deposits. As the tumor grows, it presses and causes inflammation on vital systemic nerve cells in the brain. That is why you have headaches. I was unable to get the neurologist in to speak to you today because he had to rush to surgery. He will be coming in later to discuss treatment options."

The doctor was stunned at Johnston's quickness to lead the family in prayer. He did not have time to remove himself from the room and didn't want to appear rude, so he stayed. The room echoed with amens and hallelujahs. The doctor was shocked when he heard them praying for him as well. To Gary, the test result was horrific news, and he was in no mood for praying. He impolitely removed himself from the room. The doctor wished he could do the same, but he felt a nudge on his heart to stay until the prayer was over. Dr. Hubbard had seen miracles before, but in his mind, there was a logical explanation for everything. He knew there was no other way but surgery for Erica, and by the size of the tumor, if she didn't have the surgery soon, she could be paralyzed for the rest of her life. There were always some risks in surgeries, but in Erica's case, they were unsure whether the tumor was benign or malignant. Opening her brain could cause the sack to erupt, and that meant permanent damage and possible memory loss.

After the prayer ended, and the room settled, Nolan, Greg, and Roderick went down to the hospital cafeteria to get something to eat before heading back home. Gary drove the car in silence. He did not interact or discuss with the boys what was going on with their mother. When they got home, Nolan took it upon himself to reassure Greg and Roderick that their mom was going to be fine. "I will always be truthful about what I know. I will never keep you in the dark. I don't know what's going on with Dad, but I will talk to him tomorrow and see how he is feeling about all of this."

~

Back at the hospital, Johnston was preparing to leave for church. Tonight, was Bible study, and he had to open the sanctuary. Although his thoughts were to continue to do the will of God, his mind stayed on Erica during most of the night. Erica's parents had gone to the hotel, but they went to pick up the boys from the house. Erica requested it because she knew Gary wasn't functioning well. Gary looked somber and had seemingly aged overnight. For the first time in his life, he was lost, but not because he loved her and would miss her. It was because he didn't want to be alone and responsible for everything.

Gary had always been a distinguished-looking man—six feet two inches tall, a muscular guy, and sexy to Erica. He began to gray when he turned forty, and it made him look even more handsome. They always looked perfect together, but lately, Gary didn't think so. He wanted a trophy, like his mistress. It wasn't until his trophy left him for another man that he realized he had never known what he wanted in the first place. He was heartbroken when his mistress left him, and he never once thought about Erica's feelings when his ego was being broken.

Gary was not sorry about his infidelity, and it was only by the grace of God that Erica accepted his dishonest excuse. She had every right to leave the marriage, but she didn't. Gary was terrified at the thought of Erica going through surgery, but his thoughts were on what he would have to do for her if she didn't come out of this surgery fully functioning. They only had two weeks to decide what they were going to do. If they opted to do the chemotherapy, there was no guarantee that the tumor would shrink. If the tumor grew any larger, she would risk paralysis and possibly a premature death.

At the age of forty-three, Erica only thought of her children and was led by the Holy Spirit to fast and pray for an answer. At the end of her fifth day of fasting, her body was weak, but God had confirmed her decision. She felt peace and believed she was in God's hands.

As her strength returned, Erica was able to make a visit to see her friend.

"Hello Johnston."

"Well, well. What a great surprise. Why didn't you tell me you were up and about? I would have come to see you." He got up from his chair and kissed her on the cheek.

"I needed to get out of that house."

"Oh! Is Gary not acting right?"

She hesitated to answer for a moment and thought, 'If only Gary would act right, I probably wouldn't be here.' "Actually, no. It's the boys. They're hovering over me like I'm an infant. I sent them off to the movies with my dad. That gave me a few hours to myself, so I decided to come over. I do apologize. I should have called before I came."

"Don't mention it. In any case, I've been doing a lot of praying this week. I've been asking God to send His healing power to you. It just so happened when you walked up, I was going to give you a call, and here you are. To be straight and to the point, I believe God wants you to go through with the surgery."

Erica had already decided to have the surgery. Gary had left on a two-week trip to God knows where, so she had to make the decision on her own. She smiled as God had sent a second to her motion through Johnston.

"God is so awesome. I came over here to tell you that I was going to have the surgery and to ask a big favor. I want you to be there with the boys. I know they are going to need someone around who is positive, realistic, faithful, and encouraging, and I can't count on Gary to be that for them right now. They are looking to their father to be the man he is supposed to be, but I have to admit that he hasn't been that for a very long time. They don't just need someone to be there to pray for them, they need someone they can talk to, who will be their friend if it's my time to leave this earth.

"I can do that. Do you think Gary would mind if I took the boys for a couple of days? Our church is going on a camping trip this weekend. They can come with us.

Erica chuckled. "Gary is gone for two weeks, so you don't have to worry about him."

The look on Johnston's face said it all. "You mean to tell me that Gary left you to go through all of this on your own? You have got to be kidding me!?"

"I am sorry to say this, but I am not kidding. He left on Sunday night with a few of his buddies. I didn't stop him because ultimately, this is between me and God. I don't need negativity around me right now, anyway."

"Well, don't worry about a thing. The boys will be taken care of."

Erica smiled from ear to ear. "That sounds great. I talked to the doctor, and they are scheduling the surgery for next week. Dr. Hubbard is supposed to call me tomorrow with the details."

"Good. So, let the boys know that I will pick them up Friday after school. Just stay prayerful and rest as much as you can."

Her smile always had an influence on him smiling too. He couldn't resist wanting to make Erica happy in any way without committing sin. They had truly become friends this time, and he didn't want anyone to think he was coveting another man's wife. But God knew his heart.

Over the weekend, Erica had the house to herself. Nolan protested going camping while his mother was sick, but Erica and Nolan's girlfriend Marie talked him into going. Marie was a lovely girl who was respectful to Nolan's parents and had a great deal of self-respect. She was strong-willed but not bossy or demanding. Erica could see them getting married, but she really didn't want to think about it too much. That would mean becoming a grandmother.

Erica continued to prefer the idealistic point of view that she wanted all her boys to finish college before they got hitched and made a family of their own. She wanted them to be responsible young men and to truly love their wives. She often told them, "All of you will make mistakes in life but know that God is always there to help you get up. You must allow God to work in your life and most of all, learn from your mistakes."

At their age, Nolan and Greg knew only one thing for sure. They would never say it, but they planned to work hard and make sure they didn't turn out to be like their fathers. The boys were now twelve, fourteen, and seventeen. For a while, they were able to forget about their mother's illness and enjoy the festivities at camp. It wasn't until the evening time when everything was quiet that they prayed to God, hoping their mother was okay.

Roderick adored his father and prayed for him the most. He wanted Gary to be like he used to be—a fun-loving dad who admired his son's tenacity and courage to be a daredevil. Roderick would try anything, especially things his brothers were too afraid to do.

They were all different in their own way—Nolan was the athlete, Greg was the academic whiz, and little Roderick was the stuntman and athlete, and academic whiz. Erica wondered what her sons would become; she prayed they would be happy living for God and living a life of their dreams.

Erica sat in her white-and-black plush living room. The African paintings that hung on her wall were exquisite and refined. Her home was her castle. She reclined in the plush black leather chaise and waited for the boys to arrive from their camping trip. Erica's mother was in the kitchen cooking dinner while Erica rested and listened to John P. Kee sing, 'My Healing.'

~

The next morning, Erica went under heavy sedation. The prepping nurse had already cut the hair away from the area where the saw would be used to cut open the space. As that portion of the surgery was complete, an incision was made to open a hole to reach the sac.

"Jesus!" Dr. Stein quickly moved his hands away.

"What is it, Dr. Stein?" Dr. Hubbard asked as he was sitting in the observation deck. Dr. Stein looked up at Dr. Hubbard and then to nurse Joan.

"The tumor has shrunk to half the size it was before."

"What! How can that be? She hasn't taken any chemo!"

"Dr. Hubbard, I've never seen anything like this in the thirty years I've been doing these surgeries."

"It was God," Dr. Hubbard said with such adoration and conviction in his voice. "It was God who caused the tumor to shrink. There's no other explanation. As far as I am concerned, it is no accident that all of us in this room have witnessed this today."

Dr. Hubbard had been seeking what he didn't know how to find, but it was the seed that Johnston had planted while ministering to him in the hospital cafeteria as they got coffee. Johnston could not have had any idea that Dr. Hubbard would be in the operating room with Erica. Dr. Stein and everyone else were stunned by Dr. Hubbard's words, but as he plainly put it, they could not come up with a logical explanation as to why the sack was half the size it was two weeks ago. The surgery was a complete success, and the sack was removed without any signs of neurological damage. As long as no infection set in, Erica would fully recover and would be able to go home soon.

It would be several weeks before Erica would be able to get out of the hospital, and several weeks before she was able to get out of the house. Gary worked as much as he could to avoid having to interact with Erica. The boys would come in every morning to say goodbye before they left for school, and they would come to see her as soon as they got home.

Gary was only attentive to her basic needs, but there was not much conversation between the two. Erica knew they would have to talk soon. Something had to change.

Chapter 6

It Will Make Sense Later

DREAMING IN HER TIME OF HEALING, she was a beautiful queen named Sonia with colored skin that only the sun could make. She had an hourglass figure, and gold surrounded her. She had a handsome king with a dark complexion and full lips. He was muscular but not overbearing. The subjects of their kingdom were sworn to secrecy, bound by a solemn oath that if they crossed the king or queen's throne, their lives would become more worthless than donkeys pulling the dung to fertilize the fields. The kingdom belonged to them, and they ruled over what God had blessed them to have and what the elders allowed.

Queen Sonia's husband was King Jabo Canoo, and he was mainly used for appearances. She loved him with all her heart, but the two kept that truth a secret. They were friends as well as lovers, and they did not plan to be in love. They cherished every sacred moment spent alone together. In the public eye, in the company of the dignitaries doing business for the kingdom, they treated each other like nothing.

If Queen Sonia had total control of the kingdom, she would not have cared what others thought about her love for King Canoo, but she was only eighteen, and the king was twenty. They had only been married for a year and were forbidden to have children until she turned twenty. They waited two years to consummate their marriage. They could not risk being intimate with each other because the doctor would check to see if she was pregnant every month. It was a horrid life to live. If she did not produce any children by the age of twenty-one, the elders would order the couple to divorce and would make the queen seek another husband.

An heir was the goal of this union, and it didn't matter what gender of the child, if there was an heir to take over the throne once she turned forty-years old. At forty, the elders figured it would be too old to rule a kingdom. They believed that when a woman turned forty, her body, hormones, and demeanor would change, and the change would affect her ability to make rational decisions.

If a male heir were born, he could get married and start having children as young as sixteen, if his wife were at least twenty years old. His wife would be chosen, and if she could not have children, they would have her killed. A barren woman was considered useless—she was of no use to any man. But in the dream, Queen Sonia was different. She would live even though she did not bear any children by age twenty; the elders would spare her life because she was the only heir from her parent's union.

Queen Sonia's mother died giving birth to her, and her father was not allowed to marry anyone else. Marrying a widower was dishonorable to the previous marriage and to the heir, so it was not allowed. Once Sonia became of age to rule the kingdom, her father was ordered to go to a village where no one knew who he was. This made Sonia hate her people. The way of life was that a person—even a person of royal blood—could be separated from family and be left alone in an instant. Although handmaidens, servants, and guards surrounded her, she still felt alone. The loneliness subsided when she got married. She told her new husband the stories about her mother that her father told before the council took him away.

"My mother was beautiful and full of life. My father used to tell me that she lured him with her walk. They fell in love before they could consummate their union. My father told me that they did not even dare to kiss. My mother was shy, but she enticed my father, and he followed her lips with every word. I wish I would have known her."

"I bet she was as beautiful as you, my love. I guess when all of this is over, and we have children, they will banish us too. At least then, we could truly be together."

"What about our children? They will have to go through this horrid life without their family. Although this tradition has passed down through thousands of generations, can we honestly say that this is the way it has to be? What if we could get the council to change their minds? We are the facades of this kingdom. We don't really rule anything. The only reason I continue to be here is that I don't want to disgrace my family."

"My dearest love, you have nothing to worry about right now.

Things will change, you'll see."

But things didn't change for them. When Queen Sonia turned twenty-one and didn't have any children, the council banished her husband, and their marriage was no more. She was bitter and hated the people who made her marry another. This second marriage produced six children. Queen Sonia did not love her new husband, but she loved her children. She taught them to be individuals before they too would banish their parents from their sights.

The time came when Queen Sonia and her husband were banished by their children. Queen Sonia left her husband and ran away to find her beloved Joba. He was waiting for her all along. The love they shared never ceased, even though they were apart. Ten years later, Sonia's children proved to be too much for the council to handle. They had the knowledge she imparted to them and the wisdom God had granted them. They were smart, intelligent, and they could read. They knew that the council could not deny them the request to read the ancient scrolls. They kept most of the traditions, but they changed the laws about whom they could marry. They made it to where they could marry whomever they wanted.

The new law was a victory for all queens of the past. If they could have rallied their spirits to soar the skies above, they would have. As there was nothing new known under the sun, God made sure that Queen Sonia and her family knew who He was and what He could do if they just believed. Sonia's children ruled the kingdom and made changes to the laws that were not previously granted.

Previously, others had attempted to change the laws, but they could not read the laws and thus they were unable to change anything. But because of Sonia's children, the council was finally defeated and done away with. True leadership was up to them.

~

Erica wondered if this dream was a message from God. She wondered what it meant or if it had any meaning at all. 'Maybe it's just my imagination, and I'm having some type of mental breakdown', she thought. In that very moment, she felt peaceful. She couldn't see it or touch it, but she could feel peace and love around her; she felt ready to confront whatever would come.

Erica had been devastated when she had to reconcile with the fact that she had to forgive her husband for his infidelity. According to Gary, the infidelity was her fault because she had a sexual problem that made him not want to make love to her. It wasn't up for discussion because she felt like she didn't have a problem sexually. It was clear that she desired intimacy more than he did, and it was a slap in the face to know that he refused to have sex with her.

"Go find somebody you can dictate to on how and when you want them to make love to you," Gary would say.

This was the final straw to what she considered to be the utmost degrading thing a husband could do to his wife. Lying in bed alone, crying ferociously, she didn't even know what to pray for. She had fought so hard to keep her marriage intact, and now the intimacy that she thought would help, was also out of reach. Going crazy was not an option. Being with another man to get even was not an option. What was revealed in surgery did nothing to change how dysfunctional their marriage was and how much her husband did not want to have a relationship with her.

The following morning, she went to church. She walked in and felt the love of everyone—her family and all the believers who had been praying for her healing. Erica testified of God's goodness to her, and the Spirit of the Lord filled the sanctuary. There wasn't a dry eye in the building. As Erica shared her testimony about how her tumor had shrunk, God renewed her strength. She looked around and saw Dr. Hubbard sitting in the congregation and went over to hug him. He had found what he had been seeking, and the evidence was all over his face.

Erica couldn't help but to remember the words her husband spoke to her just the evening before. She couldn't forget how he flat-out refused to be intimate with her. Just the nastiness from the enemy to place that temptation in front of her because the first person she could think of was Johnston. She knew that she would have to stay away from him for a while to combat the enemy's devices and know that the devil was under her feet. She tried not to hate Gary, but she knew that their relationship would never be the same. She no longer desired her husband and knew that he hadn't desired her for quite some time. This was confirmation that soon he would leave Erica for good. God was preparing her, and from that day forward, Erica was at peace about the outlook of their marriage and knew that the boys would be all right. The boys were already speculating that their parents would divorce soon, but they didn't say anything.

Erica committed herself to God. He had proven Himself to her time and time again, so she saw no other option than to give all of her problems over to Him. She didn't want to ever be married again. This was her second failed marriage, and she didn't want to go through that kind of pain ever again. She was ready and willing to do what He wanted her to do. She never had to depend on Gary financially, so there would be no changes in her finances with him leaving. It would be just her and Jesus.

The day came when Gary won the lottery for four and a half million dollars. He decided right then and there that he wanted a divorce, and he left the same day and moved into a hotel. Erica didn't want anything from him, except college funds set up for each of the boys. Other than that, she asked for nothing. It was finally time for her to work on herself and live.

The boys had 1.2 million dollars between them, and she would take no less than that in the divorce settlement. Erica knew Gary well enough to know that the money wouldn't last long. It was like that scene from The Color Purple, where the woman pointed her two fingers at her husband and said, "Until you do right by me, everything you even think about gonna fail!" It was just that simple; she felt like she didn't have to do anything to set things straight. She remembered the scripture: *"What does it profit a man to gain the entire world and lose his soul?"* Well, Gary had lost his soul a long time ago, but it wasn't evident until four years later when Erica received a phone call learning that he had a massive heart attack. His lottery lifestyle had taken a toll on him.

Chapter 7

God's Word Is Yay and Amen

ERICA DROVE THE BOYS TO SEE GARY. Greg and Roderick were silent the entire way there. Roderick was the most distraught of all the boys. Erica prayed they would forgive their father. It took Erica a while to do so but she was an adult and understood what forgiveness meant. Her sons on the other hand, were teenagers looking for their father to be their hero. How would this affect them in the long run? Nolan couldn't leave school during his midterms, but he convinced me to take the boys to go see Gary. Nolan always looked at things differently.

> Erica's journal entry:
> I was petrified to see what had become of the man I was supposed to be in love with. I didn't even want to see him because he had hurt my boys. I had forgiven him without an ounce of "I told you so, Gary" in my mind. But I doubted that even this situation would soften his heart to accept Christ in his life.

I let Greg and Roderick to go into the hospital room alone. I don't wish sickness on anyone. I felt bad for Gary, but I wasn't ready to see him just yet. It made me reminisce back to when I was in my first marriage. How much I hated and wanted him dead. I knew after repenting for my thoughts about him, I certainly didn't want to have those thoughts again.

Sixteen-year-old Roderick came out of the room sobbing. Greg consoled him.

"Mom, he looks really bad. I don't think it was just a heart attack. He looks old and tormented. He doesn't look the same. I don't think he will ever look the same." Roderick grabbed Erica and wouldn't let her go. "Momma, I don't want you to go in there. I want you to remember how he was before," Roderick said.

"Greg, I want you to take Roderick down to the cafeteria, and you guys go find something to eat. Then go wait in the car for me. I really don't want to go in there to see your father, but I think I should. I shouldn't be long, but I want you to wait in the car for me and don't come back up here. Do you understand?"

"Yes ma'am." They both turned and walked away.

It was hard for Erica to see Gary like that. Not only did he have a massive heart attack, but he had a mild stroke as well. The boys were right; Gary didn't look like himself at all. He looked like his elderly father lying in the bed, but it was Gary.

Gary was awoken and talked with a slur. Erica took a seat next to him. He reached for her hand and squeezed it. It hurt her heart to see him like this because she remembered the vibrant man Gary once was.

"Can you hear me?" he began to speak. "I never could fool you, Erica, and so I will not try now. I admit that I played you for almost four years. I slept around with other women and blew so much money."

Erica grabbed his hand. "Gary, what are you trying to say?"

"What I'm trying to say is that I've lost everything. I have enough to pay my doctor's bills, but other than that, I am broke." Erica didn't know what to say, so she let him continue to tell his pitiful story. "I lost $500,000 alone just in gambling, and now I am paying the price. What I want to ask is if I could move back in for a while or borrow some of the boys' college fund until I get back on my feet."

'Oh, no', she thought. It wasn't enough that he allowed the devil to tear our family apart. His health was in the balance, and life or death was hanging over his head, but this devil still has the audacity to want more. I've forgiven him for all he's done, but now he is messing with my children's future!

"Gary, I came here to tell you that this is a warning, and the next time you will lose your life. Give your life over to God and be free. God loves you. You must repent and accept Him to be your Lord and Savior." Erica walked out of the hospital room and never looked back.

~

She had to move to a place where Gary couldn't hurt her family anymore. She had to get out of California. Erica was going to miss her church home and the house she bought with Gary, but she knew that something had to change. She promised the boys they would like Georgia. Atlanta would be their new home.

It would take a while to sell the house and figure out what they would keep and what they would sell. Johnston came by often to check on Erica and the boys.

"Erica, promise me you're not just running away from your past. Why do you want to move to Atlanta?"

"I'm not running away from anything," Erica replied to Johnston. "Gary had a stroke and a heart attack a few months ago. The boys and I went to the hospital to see how he was doing. He's broke and had the nerve to ask if he could move back in or borrow money from the boys' trust fund. I couldn't believe he would ask me that. He has siblings here who can help take care of him. Why would he want to take money from his children? That's why I am moving. To protect my boys. He hurt them before, and I won't let him do it again. I put ten thousand dollars in his account so that he can support himself when he gets out of the hospital. He has that and my prayers, and he can get on disability, but that's all he gets from me. I don't want Gary trying to wiggle his way back into our lives again.

"I never told you about the time when Greg and Roderick visited Gary the weekend after he won the money. He took them to his brand-new home in Laguna Niguel and just left them there the entire weekend. He wouldn't come home until four or five in the morning and was gone by noon the next day. The boys came back home so mad. They didn't talk to their dad for months after that. Gary sent them all kinds of gifts through the mail to apologize. After our divorce was final, Gary did the same thing when the boys visited him. Then as time went by, he stopped sending them gifts and calling.

One time he didn't call them for six whole months. Johnston, I can't keep putting my boys through all that foolishness. I know that it's only going to get worse because he has not changed and doesn't seem like he wants to change. All he wants is sympathy because he's a user. Tough love is all I can give him. I have compassion for his illness, and I will continue to pray for his salvation, but I have to protect my children and let him go. If he gets his life in order, then I will welcome him back into my sons' lives, but only then. And he can forget about ever being my husband again.

"I've been offered a position as a court investigator at the Superior Court of Georgia. They are paying me a stipend for travel there and back. Once the house is sold, we'll be moving to Atlanta. We're going there in a couple of weeks to look at some houses. I was wondering if you would like to go with us?"

"Wow! I would be honored. I just need a couple of weeks to arrange caregiving services for my parents and to let the pastor know that I'll be out of town."

"I know you have a lot of responsibility here with your parents and the church. I don't want to interfere with that, but the boys and I would love your company."

"I would love to, Erica." Johnston grabbed and hugged her.

"Thank you, Johnston. I will cover everything. In any case, if you don't feel comfortable with that, you can pay me back. I want to make sure our reservations are the same, and we can leave and arrive together."

"That's fine. I will pay you back though."

"I figured you'd say that. Anyhow, how are your parents?"

"They are doing well. Of course, they are up in age, but overall, their health is great, and they have been able to take a couple of local trips and have a good time."

"How have you been dealing with everything?"

"Well, to tell you the truth, it has been trying. It's not that they are a bother, but it's a lot on my plate. They have their own money, but I am responsible for taking care of their finances. I make sure they are being paid properly, and I take them to the bank when they need to go. Being responsible for my parents and the church takes up all my time. I feel like my life is on hold. I would like to remarry, but I'm not sure how that would work out with all my responsibilities."

"Johnston, have you ever thought that maybe God does not want us to remarry? We spend so much time thinking about our lives with spouses and children that we don't appreciate our relationship with God enough. Nolan is away at college now, but when I had all three boys, I was always busy with games, clubs, and church activities. I didn't have much time left over to build a strong relationship with God. My problems with Gary drove me to seek God more, but now I have more time to seek Him for me. I envy people like you who are in full-time ministry. Your job is to seek God. I know that the ministry has its own problems, but I would rather be in your shoes. I don't understand why you would want to add a spouse to your plate."

"Erica, you are not the first person to say that, but God said in His word that He will give you the desires of your heart. I do desire to be married. I seek God's will, and if He doesn't send her, then I don't want her. But I do desire companionship with a woman who loves and serves God as much as I do. I want someone to be there for me. Darn it, I want to have sex again."

The mood of the room was a bit awkward, but they laughed, and it lightened the atmosphere. They both tried to figure out what they wanted to eat for dinner. Erica and Johnston felt comfortable with each other and realized that they were friends and were much closer than they had ever been before. They could tell the truth without offending each other. Her children respected Johnston even more than their own father, and it didn't take long for Roderick to realize that his dad was no good for his mother. After the long battle in deciding what they wanted to eat for dinner, they chose Chinese food. They went to the Twin Dragons restaurant and sat down to continue their conversation over dinner.

Chapter 8

No Accident

REMEMBERING THE HURT GARY CAUSED in her life and the lives of her children. She remembered the chaos that was so rampant in her home. She wondered how she made it through each day. During those times, she felt alone and feared what the next day would bring. She thought about how her faith had been tested and tried and how God was the only one who could bring her through. Tears fell down her face and stained her pillow at night. She managed to stay strong and think about the overwhelming support of her parents. Their age was a factor in her deciding to move to Atlanta, Georgia. She had wanted to move closer to her parents long before now, but Roderick had been attached to his father for so long, and it would take time for him to understand that they needed to be away from him.

Erica held on to her faith and trusted that God would work things out. She had to depend on Him to see her through everything that was going on in her life. Johnston was the companion she needed, and that support she couldn't find anywhere else. She knew that his life was in Los Angeles. God had placed him in a strong, innovative ministry—one that does outreach and helps people in need. The senior pastor, Benjamin Morgan, was very wise and only five years older than Johnston.

Moving to Atlanta was no accident. It was God's plan, and Erica just rode along. What was ahead for her? What would she have to face tomorrow? Her children were doing well; she had no complaints about their behavior, schoolwork, or social life. They weren't out drinking, smoking, or doing drugs. They had grown up to become respectable young men with bright futures. She urged them to keep their eyes on God and look for Him to fulfill His promises in their lives. Erica would read Proverbs 1:1–33 to them and believed that they would give their lives over to the Lord. Her sons prayed and enjoyed going to church, but they had not fully committed to God. Atlanta was a notable change from Los Angeles, but without a doubt, Erica knew this was where she was supposed to be. Johnston was a constant reminder of the man she was supposed to marry; she could never get that truth out of her head. Johnston never hesitated to drop whatever he was doing to speak to Erica on the phone. "How are you doing out there?"

"It is unimaginable. I haven't been in snow since I was in the seventh grade living in Philadelphia. Back then it was fun, but now, oh my goodness! I feel like I'm going to freeze to death. But it melts quickly. I'm guessing the weather where you are is beautiful."

"Well, today was seventy-eight degrees, and this is supposed to be winter."

"Johnston, you know this is the sign of the Lord's return, when we aren't able to tell the seasons apart. Can you believe we are seeing the manifestation of God's Word at hand? I get excited when I think about it. You know, it's scary and exciting at the same time."

"I know what you mean. So how are you doing?"

"We are doing well. The boys are adjusting. I have no complaints. I was promoted to a new position a month ago. I like it a lot. Investigating has been a blast so far. I came at a good time; they will be out for the summer in a few months. I am managing my time wisely."

"It sounds like you are moving on."

"Johnston, you know me well enough to know that you can't keep a good woman down for too long."

"So how are your neighbors?"

"Oh, they have been wonderful. But I am concerned about my neighbor next door to me. Occasionally, I see him peeking at me from his living room window, and he quickly closes the curtain when I notice him. During the day, he doesn't come out at all. One night, I saw him coming out of the door as I was taking out the trash. He turned off his porch light but then turned it back on after he rushed back inside and closed the door. He's just weird. The neighbors say that he has been like that for years. Ever since his wife died, he has his groceries delivered. They say he goes on long walks at night in the wooded part of the neighborhood. I don't know, Johnston. I don't know if he is just a hermit or a real nut case that can't come out in public."

"Well, just stay prayerful and safe. He could very well be harmless or trying to hide something."

"That's what I'm concerned about. Anyway, when are you coming back out to visit?"

"I don't know. My father is ill, and we don't know how long he has left to live. His kidneys are shutting down. Right now, they are only functioning at 40 percent. My parents are praying for an answer on whether to put him on dialysis or just allow God to take him home. They don't want to discuss it with me. This is a decision they want to make on their own."

Although Johnston's parents made the decision to try dialysis, his father still passed away a year later. Johnston was saddened by the loss of his father, but he took comfort in knowing that his father was in a better place. Mr. Matthews was eighty-six years old and lived a great life. He traveled around the world with his wife doing ministry and mission work. Erica considered Mr. Matthew's life to be a testimony and proof that doing God's work is the best thing a person can achieve in life. A year later, eighty-three-year-old Mrs. Matthews passed away. Erica and the boys flew back and forth to California and attended both funerals.

Johnston was appreciative of Erica's support during the time he lost his parents. He did not feel alone; Erica helped him prepare for both funerals. Johnston always had her back whenever she needed him, so it was good for him to know that she had his back too. Greg and Roderick always enjoyed returning back to California, which was their home state, even if it was for just a few days. With Nolan's athletic schedule, it was hard for him to get away unless there was an emergency in the immediate family.

Nolan played baseball. He called Erica to let her know that he would be playing in Atlanta and that he would send tickets to the family—Johnston included. He was a proud Stanford Cardinal man who had graduated with honors.

"The game is next week."

Both Greg and Roderick responded as though they had a choice to go to the game.

"I'm free," one said.

"So am I," said the other.

Erica looked at both. "What makes you think you had a choice in the matter?"

Greg put his arms around Erica, and Roderick joined in. "Aww, Mom! Come on. Don't take it like that. You know that we will always go to Nolan's games."

"Well, anyway, he said he has something to tell us when he gets here. This will be your opportunity to tell Nolan that you have been accepted to Georgia Tech School of Physics for your master's program. He'll be so proud of you."

"Come on, Mom. Stop being mushy."

"You have no idea how proud I am of you, do you?"

"Mom, I know that you are proud of me."

"There is no doubt in my mind that you will do well, as long as you keep God first. Have you decided on a career to pursue?"

"I'm looking into biomedical engineering."

"Well, once you become that, then you can tell me what that is. Until then, keep your brain to yourself."

"Oh! That was funny. That was really funny."

"You know what? To be honest, I am so glad you are excelling academically, but what's more important to me is that you are normal. You know what you want, and you're not afraid of being the genius that you are. But you still know how to throw a football and have fun in life. A career is important, but you have to remember to study your Bible and live according to God's will, not your own. Lots of people don't believe in science, and lots of scientists don't believe in God. You will be tested and tried in your field. You never know what's around the corner, but God knows, and He will direct your footsteps if you acknowledge Him. I love you!"

"Okay. I love you too, Mom."

~

The sunshine reigned supreme. It was not a beaming heat but a warmth that only God could regulate. On Erica's street, peace and quiet with nothing but birds chirping was unheard of. There were no car horns blowing, and no school buses driving by. At six-thirty in the morning, there was nothing but peace and quiet on the block of Amsterdam and Fifth. The tree leaves whistled their morning song and brought the reality of the westward winds. She turned on her car, read the sixth chapter of Judges, and took off to work. It was no longer a struggle to wake up and bless God for His grace and mercy. Erica's conviction to stay in the Lord's will was strong, but with every step toward seeking God, the trials in her life also increased.

~

Erica's job was far from typical. She quickly advanced in the ranks and became a trainer for the Court Investigators of Homicides (CIH). As a CIH Trainer, she trained employees to collect and preserve evidence to complete investigative assignments; present at hearings, court proceedings, and conferences; examine books, records, and accounts relative to homicide investigations; prepare reports of investigation; testify in cases involving homicides; review prior history of arrests, character, and employment records of defendants; serve subpoenas and other legal processes; review crime scenes; and gather and evaluate facts from evidence and from police, agents, witnesses, and other sources. As a CIH Trainer, she acted in a lead capacity for subordinate investigators.

Erica constantly thought about Johnston. Their past always reminded her of how much God had changed her for the better. She used her experiences with sexual immorality to help men and women work through their personal problems. The trials of her past changed her outlook on helping others who did not know the Lord as their personal Savior and those who knew Him but were struggling to let go of their past indiscretions.

Erica had a coworker named Tevin, whom she had never met, but had only heard about him. Tevin was an intelligent, creative, and handsome Christian man who had not yet submitted to God and His will. An opportunity came for Tevin and Erica's paths to cross. Of all places, they met in the elevator. Alone in the elevator, he said her name, and she responded, "Hello."

"How are you doing? We've never met, but I have heard so much about you and the work you're doing on the tenth floor."

Erica put out her hand to shake his. "Well, thank you so much. What's your name?"

"I'm sorry. My name is Tevin. I have heard so much about you, and now I finally get to meet you in person."

"So, Tevin, how are things going down there on the fifth floor?"

"It's going great. I have a high-profile case coming my way. I know that it's going to be a circus for a while."

The elevator doors opened. "Well, this is my floor. It was nice meeting you, Tevin. See you around sometime."

Tevin hesitated, but then he walked out behind Erica. "I'm actually getting off on your floor anyway. I need to talk to your boss. Do you mind if I stop by your office after I get through talking to Stephenson?"

"No, not at all. As a matter of fact, my office is right next to his. You'll see my name on the door. If I'm not in my office, ask my assistant, Caroline. She'll find me."

"Will do."

After Tevin talked to Stephenson, he went to find Erica. He wasted no time, "See, Erica, I'm a believer." He waited for her to respond. Her silence puzzled him.

"No offense for asking, but you are a believer in what?"

He smiled and almost laughed. "I'm a believer in Christ, just like you."

"Oh! I thank God for that. What is it you want to talk to me about?"

"Let me just say it. I was talking to someone in confidence, another judge. I was telling him my situation, and he told me to talk to you. He said that you were a great person to talk to for spiritual advice."

"Tevin, I'd be happy to talk to you, but first I have to ask you a question. It's great to know that you believe in Jesus, but have you accepted Him as your Lord and personal Savior? Are you living a holy and separated life in Christ? Because if you are not, then this conversation you want to have with me will be pointless unless you have allowed God to take over your life. I say this because godly wisdom and understanding comes from God, not me."

"Let me make it plain to you. The trouble started when I accepted Christ. Because of my job, it's hard to sit in a church service. My pager and cellphone go off all the time, and I need to respond to those calls because of arraignments and all. I am only thirty years old, but I have been here for five years. I love this job, and I know God blessed me with it. It was my desire to work for the justice of people. I grew up in church. My father was a minister, and my mother was a missionary. Like I said, my troubles really started after I recommitted myself during New Year's last year."

"Well, what's going on?"

"I am really having trouble in my relationships with women. I have had two girlfriends in the past four months, and both have turned out the same. I have struggled with fornication and have not been able to abstain."

"Tevin, I hope whoever recommended you talk to me told you I am strictly by the book, with compassion of course. I am no longer ashamed of my past, and that is why I can share what I've experienced and what God allowed me to go through. Now what I have to say may sound harsh, but I only speak the truth. First and foremost, you know the scriptures. You know what you must do to abstain from sex. Stop putting yourself in situations where you know you will mess up. If she's at your place, and you guys are kissing on the couch, it is likely that things will lead to other things. You know you have a problem with abstaining, so just stop putting yourself in those situations where you are weak. The enemy knows your weaknesses, and he is using what he knows to keep you bound by fornication. I know you believe in Christ, but you have not made a true commitment to the Lord. When you commit to Christ, you will learn the enemy's tactics. You will learn how to avoid being put into situations that lead to sin. Two relationships in the past four months is nothing good. Maybe you're looking for a woman to complete you, but only God can do that."

"I know, but I have known these women for many years. Each one of them, I thought that God had sent to me. The girl I'm currently dating wants to move in with me after two and a half months of dating."

"Tevin, the writing is on the wall. What's wrong with the picture? Once you have accepted Christ, you are no longer your own. You have been bought with a price. A true believer and follower of Christ will read, study, and live to obey the commandments of God. First Samuel 15:22 says, *What is more pleasing to the Lord: your burnt offerings and sacrifices or your obedience to His voice?'* It also says in John 10:27: *'My sheep know my voice, and a stranger they will not follow.'* Tevin, you must be in a place where you can hear God's voice and feel His Spirit leading and guiding you down the path. If Satan can get you distracted with the cares of life, then he can keep you away from God. I'm going to write down some scriptures for you, and I want you to read them. Read Romans 12:1, 1 Peter 5:7, 1 Thessalonians 5:16, John 15:16, 1 John 1:9, Philippians 4:13, 2 Peter 1:10, and 2 Corinthians 13:5. There are many scriptures I can give you, but these encompass an understanding that God chose you for a purpose. Your purpose is to go through things in order to glorify God through your own testimony. Have you talked to your father about this?"

Tevin stood up and started to pace the floor. "No, Erica. I can't go to my father about this. I need some answers."

"First, you have to examine yourself and determine if you really want to change. You sound like you have a little rebellion in you when it comes to your father, and there are some underlining issues that need to be addressed. If you don't address them, your relationship with God will continue to suffer. You also need to repent for your sexual immorality and truly seek God for the answers you are looking for. The last question I have is when was the last time you fasted, prayed, and read your Bible?"

"To be honest, I haven't read the Bible since before I met my new girlfriend. I haven't prayed in weeks, and the only time I've fasted was when I was younger."

"God is understanding and forgiving, and He has provided you with the necessary tools to make it in this life. You are renewed in Christ, and God wants you to recommit to Him. He is a jealous God, and you have put sex over Him. But He has not forsaken or left you. So, the choice is up to you to make God first in your life. He has put you in a great position of judgment through law and fairness. You have a belief in God that many other judges don't have, and you are only thirty-two years old. God wants to increase your faith for you to have the abundant life He has promised in His word. Recognize the gift God has placed in you. The Word of God says, 'A man that finds a wife finds a good thing.' God created you to be with a woman that He has ordained for you. The Bible says in Matthew 6:33: 'Seek ye first the kingdom of God and His righteousness, and all things shall be added to you.' It did not say that God would add only some things you need. It said that He would add all things you need according to God's will. He is not going to make you see things differently. You have to want His will to take over and direct your path daily. Don't ever let anyone tell you that you are not going to have trials and tribulations. As sure as the day is long, you will be a target for the enemy's attacks. He will try and sway you to believe that God is not who He says He is."

"I've heard this before. I understand what you are saying."

"Well, then that means God has sent me to confirm. You should also know a warning comes before destruction. Always remember Satan desires to devour your soul, and he doesn't want you to stop and look at the big picture."

"So, what should I do about my relationship?" Erica came from around her desk.

"Tevin, you know what you need to do. It's not like you don't know the way. Asking God for forgiveness is the easiest thing you can do if you're sincere about it. Then, you need to talk to your girlfriend about your feelings and convictions and return to the Lord and be honest about what you're struggling with. Remember, you are open for any and everything when you are not seeking God fervently through His Word and prayer. You need to pray that God fills the void you were trying to fill with sex. Also, you need to pray and ask God for guidance and direction in choosing a future helpmeet. Trust me when I say that the ultimate mistake you can make is to marry someone that God has not sent and who is unequally yoked with you. In these cases, God still honors marriage, but it will be hell before He makes things right. It is a wonderful experience when you can share common spiritual worship and reach higher heights and deeper depths in God with each other. I hope that this talk has helped you. I would like to pray with you before we go home in about twenty minutes."

"Absolutely. I'd appreciate that. Thank you for your candid guidance and for taking the time to speak to me. To tell you the truth, I felt like I was losing my mind. I know what I should be doing; I just haven't been doing it. It's about meaning what I say and doing it God's way and not my own."

Tevin and Erica prayed together for about fifteen minutes. They forged a bond in the courthouse setting that was scarcely seen. They stood on the Word of God that states where there are two or three gathered in His name, God's in the midst.

~

Back at home, Erica's thoughts stayed on the secretiveness of her neighbor. That same evening, sirens rang loud and lights shined bright as a young girl was reported missing two blocks away from Erica's home. At dusk, Roderick found out the missing girl was from down the street.

"Roderick, do you know the girl?"

"Well, she goes to my school, and I think she is new. Josh lives next door to her and says her family moved here from Virginia a month ago. She was a Caucasian female, sixteen years of age, and very shy."

Erica was shocked at Roderick's response. "Wow are you trying to follow in your mom's footsteps?"

"God, I hope so, but only the good parts. The bad stuff, I'd rather skip." Before Erica could respond, Roderick broke in. "I know, I know. There will be trials and tribulations. I just have to trust in God to make it through."

Erica pinched his cheeks. "I am so proud. My son has been listening to me."

"Mom, I love you, but you can be goofy sometimes."

"Rick just be careful. We don't know if this is an isolated incident. So, until this can be cleared up, I want you to come to my office after practice."

"Sure, I'll have Josh drop me off."

"By the way, how is practice going?"

"Aw man, in all this commotion, I forgot to tell you. Well, I have some good news and some other good news or bad news, depending on how you take it. Which do you want first?"

"Give me the good news first, so that it will override the bad or good depending on how I take the news."

"Let me get my southern, saloon Texan voice going. Whoa doggie, I passed my SATs with a 1950."

"Oh my, that is so great! Now you can go to any university you want."

"I found out at school today. They announced it over the PA system. I should get an official notice in the mail tomorrow. The other good or bad news from me is that I am being scouted by a college in California—two colleges as a matter of fact."

"And what two colleges are these?"

"Apparently, USC and UCLA have been following my career since my last year of middle school. My coach told me yesterday to let you know it may get a little crazy."

"Rick, you have a tough mom. We'll discuss this over the weekend. If I need to call in some backup, I will. For now, keep your mind on what's important and make sure you're taking precautions at school. We'll worry about what college you're going to when you're closer to the end of the school year. I am so proud of you and can't wait to ship you off."

"Mom, that's cold."

Erica continued to finish dinner. "You know, Johnston's coming tomorrow."

Roderick picked up a turkey meatball. "Great, are you going to pick him up?"

"Actually, he's going to come to my office. So, when you get out of school, come straight there so I can bring both of you home."

Roderick sat on the countertop. "Why is he coming tomorrow?"

"They're having a minister's convention, and his pastor is sending him. He'll be here all week."

"I hope you two get to have some fun while he's here. Since Nolan and Greg have been gone, you don't go out as much."

"That's because it's just you and me, kiddo. I have to make sure you're safe. I've shipped two grown sons off to college, and with God's continued help, I can ship off my last handsome son. So, don't worry about me having fun right now because as soon as you're out of here, I'm going to party like it's 1999."

They both laughed hysterically until it hurt.

"Mom, I'm going down to Josh's to see if there's any news."

"Okay. I know you're grown and all that, but call me when you get down there. Call me when you are on your way back, and don't make me come look for you, Roderick Isaiah Manning."

Roderick kissed her on the cheek. "Yes, mother dearest."

Chapter 9

Revelation

J OHNSTON WALKED INTO THE COURT BUILDING and asked for Erica. She answered, "Erica Vaughn."

"Ms. Vaughn, we have a Johnston Matthews in the lobby."

"Thank you. Give him a visitor's sticker and let him know I will be right down."

The guard hung up with a heavy hand. "Mr. Matthews, Ms. Vaughn will be right down." The guard stood there and stared at Johnston.

"Thank you," said Johnston.

Seeing Johnston was always a pleasure for Erica. That giddy feeling hit her, like a schoolgirl crush, but she prayed all the way down ten floors. She was happy, not only with how God had blessed her but because she was at peace. Walking out of the elevator, Johnston could see the exuberant confidence in Erica's walk.

"Wow," he said under his breath.

She hugged him passionately. "Johnston, it's so good to see you. How was your flight?"

"It was fine. I'm just glad I am on solid ground."

Johnston looked back at the guard, who was still staring at him.

"Come on up. As soon as Roderick gets here, we'll leave."

Johnston's face told the story. "Why does that guard keep mad dogging me?"

Erica looked back at the guard. "Well, he is very protective. Plus, he has a little crush on me, but he is harmless."

They both stepped onto the elevator. Erica told Johnston to press ten. "That dude is scary. He has no neck. Anyway, how is Roderick?"

"He's doing great. He told me yesterday he scored 1950 on his SATs, and he is being scouted by USC and UCLA. I told him we'd talk about the detail's tomorrow. I don't know if I want him back in LA, and I don't want him with his father. He's going to be eighteen soon. I am here for advice, but ultimately this is a decision he's going to have to make."

"So far, he's been making good choices. You'll just have to trust that he will continue to do so."

"I know, Johnston. I think what I fear is his father influencing his decision. If he goes back to California, I don't want him staying with his father. Roderick was the only one who didn't want to leave in the first place, and now he has an opportunity to move back."

Johnston moved in closer to Erica, so she was able to rest her head on his shoulder. "Erica, the operative word I hear from you is fear. God has not given us the spirit of fear; you have to remember why Roderick didn't want to leave. He's the baby of the family. He loved his father because he favored him. No matter what you think may happen, he is in God's hands, and Roderick has grown up since then. He knows who his father is and why you guys left in the first place. Even if you could, you shouldn't stop him from seeing his father. That would damage your relationship with him. You never had a problem with being honest and upfront with your boys and me. Don't stop now. Whatever decision Roderick makes, let him know your feelings and concerns and that you trust his decisions. I know he's your baby, and he's the last one to leave the nest, but remember, he's been the man of the house for a few years now."

The elevator door opened swiftly. "Let's finish this conversation in my office." As they walked into the office, Johnston dropped his two bags to the floor. "Wow. This is a nice office. You must be doing well here at the courthouse."

"I was promoted last year after two years of field work. I prayed for an office position, and God opened the door. Now, I'm the director of training operations. Take a look around. The view is beautiful."

"This is awesome." He said.

"No, God is awesome. I didn't mind giving up field investigation. On special occasions, I will take on a local case. Come and sit down on the couch so we can get back to what we were talking about in the elevator."

"Yea, you have to allow him to make mistakes. One last thing: make sure he understands his education is more important than sports. Although that is his catalyst in getting a free education, it's no guarantee he's going to make it to the pros."

"Okay, enough of this. What's your schedule like tomorrow?"

"I'm free all weekend except Sunday morning. I am speaking at a conference. I want you and Roderick to be there."

"Absolutely, you know we'll be there. In any case, you're going to tell Roderick exactly what you just said to me."

"I knew that was coming." The phone rang.

"Hold on, Johnston. I have to take this call." Erica reached for the phone.

"Ms. Vaughn, this is the security desk. There is a Mr. Roderick coming up to your office."

"Thanks Jed." Erica hangs up, "The superstar is coming up."

"So why did they have you come and get me, but they just let Roderick come up by himself?"

"Don't take offense. They know Roderick, and since some recent events, they check everyone. Trust me, even though they know Roderick, he has to go through the checkpoint like everyone else. Anyway, do you want to go out to dinner, or would you rather cook?"

Johnston laughed. "I thought I was the visitor in this peach state."

"Johnston don't act like you are not familiar with the kitchen." His puppy dog eyes were a soft spot she couldn't resist.

"All right, I'll cook tonight, but you have to grace us with your wonderful breakfast."

"That's a deal." Roderick knocks on the door.

"Come in, dear. Guess who's behind door number one?"

"Hey, what's up, Johnston? How's it going?"

"It's going well, big Rick. My goodness, you have grown. Your mom has been telling me some good things."

"I know, man. I can't believe it. I may be going back to Cali. Of course, if it's God's will."

"That's what I like to hear—a brother in the Lord acknowledging God's blessings. Just keep it that way. Since I'll be here all week, you are old enough to hear about some of my war stories. Whatever decision you make, just know that your mom and I will have your back."

"I know, and I appreciate that a great deal. I'm just worried about Ms. Lady over there."

Erica had to take a call, so she didn't follow the entire conversation between Johnston and Roderick. She thought about the missing girl often, and every time she did, she would pray for her safe return. She had an opportunity to visit the girl's parents after morning worship. She figured she would be able to share the gospel of Jesus Christ and to give comfort and support to the family, answering any questions she could about the legalities.

Erica was never one to sugarcoat a situation like this. If there was no note left or ransom call made within forty-eight hours of the missing report, then it was the custom to assume the child either ran away or was abducted. There was still no call made the following Friday, and the FBI had taken over the case, assuming the girl had been abducted without a trace. There were no signs of missing articles of clothing; there was only a backpack she carried to school. None of the neighborhood children saw her with anyone when she left school. It was as though she had vanished. She was an attractive young lady, but you could tell by her pictures, she was a plain jane. With this being a new place for her with unfamiliar surroundings and very few friends, someone could have easily taken her. Everything remained in her locker, and no evidence could be collected from it. Her room had been untouched, which meant she never made it home.

The devastation of losing a child was something Erica never wanted to experience personally, but she sympathized with families and prayed for the safe return of their children. Unfortunately, there were few happy endings. In their sorrow, some parents blamed God for allowing the tragedy to happen; others grew stronger and more courageous to face the evils of this world and did everything they could to make the life of their children memorable.

~

The Minister's Conference was over at noon, and Roderick had gone over to Josh's house for the night. Johnston woke up from a nap and sat next to Erica.

"What do you want to do tomorrow since you will be leaving on Sunday?" said Erica.

"Let's see. I have an appointment with some of the ministers and should be done by noon tomorrow. Roderick told me to take you out to have some fun. I have an idea of what I want to do, but it's up to you." Johnston put his legs across Erica's legs.

"How would you like dinner and a movie?" Erica kept his legs there and began to massage them.

"I actually had something else in mind. What do you say we catch an early movie? We can come back and get all dressed up and go to dinner and a play. A pastor friend of mine gave me two tickets to a gospel play."

"That sounds great! It's been years since I've been out on a date. You know, we haven't really had enough time to talk. So how is your love life, Mr. Matthews?"

"I'm still waiting on the Lord to send me my wife. It's hard to find the right woman. It seems like the older I get, the higher my standards get. At this point, I've given up on dating just to be dating. When it happens, God will let me know. I pray I'll just know she's the one without question."

"I've been thinking about it lately since Roderick will be leaving for school pretty soon. I don't know if I've totally given up, but my mind is not on dating anyone anytime soon. Right now, my focus is on shipping off my last son to college."

"You should be very proud of what you've accomplished with the boys. It's not every day we get to hear a success story. There are more and more people willing to live in sin, but your boys still honor God with their lives. I see so many kids in church falling away right before my very eyes. Girls are not waiting, and the boys end up chasing after the American dream, which will never come for most of them because they don't want to wait on God. These kids don't want to wait anymore. They want what they want now, and they are finding ways to get it quickly. They don't understand there are consequences in life for every decision they make. I have four teenage girls at the church right now who are pregnant. Of course, you have to sit them down and take them off their leadership posts until they have their babies and reconcile their relationship with God. It's devastating for the parents and embarrassing for all parties involved. I've had to stop doing a lot of marriage counseling to focus on family counseling."

"Well, if nothing else, you can take solace in knowing you are in your calling. I appreciate you taking the boys under your wing."

"The pleasure's all mine, Erica. I've been able to visit Nolan a couple of times and have gone to a couple of his games."

"I'm proud of him too. To me, he's God's miracle child. At first, I was worried that he would never come out of that tantrum stage. To be honest, I never thought he would achieve all that he has."

~

The next day, their plans went off spontaneously and without a hitch. They were able to enjoy an evening of laughter, fun, and adult conversation. It was just like the Sunday dinner she went to at Johnston's parents' house. The play was hilarious, and they laughed the night away. Erica thought to herself that she would miss Johnston's laughter and companionship. She wanted him to stay, but the time had come when Johnston had to go to the airport to return home.

"I'm going to miss you," he said.

"Make sure you call me when you get home."

"I'll call you."

"Please do." Johnston grabbed his carry-on bag. Then he gave Erica a hug and walked on the ramp toward the plane.

Two months later, the missing girl's body was found in the Carter's Lake drain. It was determined that she had been raped and killed by strangulation and then dumped in the river. The maintenance mechanic, the one who checked the drainage site, received a clogging signal, and found the body. It was common to find dead animals blocking the drain, but a human body was something altogether different. The body had been found twenty miles from the school and twenty-one miles from Erica's home. They knew the body had been dumped, but they couldn't tell where. They tried to backtrack from the original crime scene, but it seemed like an impossible task to find more clues.

Then there was a second abduction reported a mile away from the school. In murder cases like these, when more than one report was made, the FBI would take over and this time was no different. For the family, it was agonizing and difficult to identify their daughter Esther. Her face was disfigured and unrecognizable. They identified her by recognizing a known mark on her body. They were sickened at the sight of their once beloved child.

Chapter 10

Tortuous Momentum of Malice in the Heart

THREE MONTHS BEFORE RODERICK was to graduate and be shipped off to college, their once serene living space became a madhouse. Roderick was being considered for a starting position at USC, GSU, and UCLA in NCAA basketball. At seventeen years old, he was already six-eight, smart, and good-looking.

Within the last year, the phone rang every night. Girls were constantly calling and asking for "Ricky." There was only one he was remotely interested in, and even she did not have his heart.

Prom night had come, and all the basketball jocks met at Erica's home with their dates. Roderick wanted a limo, so Erica ordered an extra stretched Hummer. Erica prayed they would have an enjoy- able time. She prayed Roderick and his friends wouldn't do anything foolish. She prayed about a lot of things. She even prayed Roderick would make the right decision on which school to attend. He would have to decide in two weeks. But she was not worried. She was proud of her boy.

"Roderick, remember to be careful and make wise decisions," Erica advised. "Respect your date. You don't want to do anything you'd regret later. And don't go anywhere alone. Take precautions to keep everyone safe. I trust you to make good choices tonight. Have fun. Your brothers wanted you to know they are very proud of you. They wanted to be here, but they are busy with finals and playoffs. I'll send them the pictures I have taken of you all. Be safe and try to get home before sunrise." Erica straightened Roderick's tie, and they hugged.

"Thanks for all of this, Mom. You can trust me to make good choices tonight. I love you."

She grabbed his neck and replied, "I love you, too."

Erica prayed the entire time Roderick was at prom. She heard him step through the door at three in the morning but didn't bother to get out of bed because she didn't want him to know she was still up waiting for his safe return. She heard him creeping up the stairs, opening her door slowly. She figured it was so he wouldn't wake her, so she kept her back turned. But then he grabbed her from behind. "We have your son," the man said. Instant terror rang over Erica's body. The man who she thought was her son hit her in the back of the head, knocking her unconscious.

After an hour passed, Erica woke up dazed and in pain. She touched the back of her head and felt a huge contusion. She ran to Roderick's room as fast as she could, but she found he had not been in his bed all night. "God help me!" Erica fell to the floor and screamed. She couldn't move. Every thought ran through her mind. She wondered who had her son and what they were doing to him. She prayed he was not hurt or being tortured. She called the limo company to ask where he was, and the man said the driver took Roderick home.

"My son has not been home," she said to the call rep. "I need to talk to that limo driver now!"

The rep asked her to hold while he transferred her to the driver.

"This is Garrett, Ms. Vaughn. Garrett Morrison."

"Hi Garrett, where did you drop off my son this morning?"

"He was the last one I dropped off. It was 3:15 a.m., and I even watched him walk to the door."

'Think, Erica', she thought. "Okay, okay. Thank you, Garrett." Erica hung up the phone. Erica tried to reason as to why this was happening to her. "God, I'm not even going to ask why because I know why." She said aloud. She looked in front of the coffee table and saw Roderick's tuxedo tie on the floor. "No!" she screamed. Tears began to roll down her face as she realized that one of her greatest fears had come to pass. Her son was gone. Erica picked up the phone to call the police.

"Emergency," the operator responded.

"I want to report a kidnapping, and I need an ambulance. Someone took my son. Someone hit me in the head! Oh, God, why?" She talked and prayed chaotically. Her head was throbbing, even as she had to answer questions when the police arrived.

"Ms. Vaughn, approximately what time was your son taken?" the officer asked.

"My son rode with the rest of his basketball team to their prom. They rode in a limo from Taylor Limo Service. I spoke to the driver this morning; his name is Garrett Morrison. He said he dropped off Roderick here last night. He said he saw him walk to the door before driving off. I found the tie my baby wore to prom. It's on the floor, and I didn't touch it." Erica pointed to the tie.

"Tell me, how did you get that bump on your head?"

"This morning, I thought I heard my son come through the door. I pretended to be asleep because I didn't want him to think I was waiting up for him. I had my back turned, so I couldn't see it was not my son coming through the door. The man grabbed me from behind and whispered in my ear, 'We have your son,' and then he hit me in the back of my head! I must have been out for some time, and when I came to, I dialed 911."

"Ms. Vaughn, we promise we will get to the bottom of this." The detective said.

As the paramedics looked Erica over, Roderick's best friend Josh appeared at the door. "Ms. Vaughn, are you, all right? Where's Roderick? Is he upstairs?"

"Joshua, someone kidnapped my baby. Did you see anyone lurking around the neighborhood last night?"

"Kidnapped? The limo driver dropped us off here. Roderick waited until I walked down the street to my house before he went in."

The detective turned to Joshua and asked him if he was sure Roderick made it into the house.

"No, sir. I am not a 100 percent sure he went in, but I saw the limo driver still there when I went in the door."

"Can you recall what time it was exactly?"

"It had to be between 2:55 and 3:10a.m. because when we got out of the limo, Ricky and I talked for about five minutes before I walked to my house."

"I'm sorry, who's Ricky?"

"That's my son's nickname. We sometimes call him Ricky for short, instead of Roderick."

"When I got to my room, it was 3:15a.m. on my clock," Josh continued.

"Hmmm, the driver said he dropped Roderick off at 3:15a.m.," said Erica.

"Erica," the detective said, "for now, I want you to let the ambulance take you to get X-rays of your contusion. We will be able to use the X-rays for evidence. We are going to get the tie analyzed and see if we can retrieve any evidence from that as well. There was no break in the door, so he had to have opened the door. Ms. Vaughn, you know the drill, you know what has to take place."

"I know, Detective Mutchison. I will leave my key with Joshua while I'm at the hospital. If the CSI team is still here when I get back, I'll stay out of the way for them to do their job. I have to make some phone calls and grab my I.D. before I leave." Erica rubbed the back of her head. Erica got on the phone and called Nolan and Greg. She called Johnston too, and he said he would be flying out the following day. Erica called Gary numerous times, but he did not pick up, so she just left messages that Roderick was missing.

Later that afternoon, Detective Mutchison returned to Erica's home, and he brought another detective with him. He saw Erica was still visibly shaken over what was happening, and he tried to comfort her the best way he could. "I'm glad everyone is gone. I'm sorry for not letting you know I was bringing someone with me, but my superior wanted Ms. Luna to come along. She is a newly recruited detective in training."

Erica shook hands with the new detective. "Hello, Ms. Luna."

"You can call me Sarai."

"Please, take a seat. Would anyone like a drink?"

"No thank you," both detectives replied in unison.

"I know you haven't had much rest, but I would like to go over what happened one more time, and then we can continue from there." Erica told the story of what happened once again. As she recounted the events, the phone rang, and she ran to answer it.

~

In another area, Roderick was being held in a cold storage space. He was tied to a chair with wheels, and he couldn't see anything because it was pitch black.

"Why are you keeping me here?" he called out. "I haven't done anything to you people." Then suddenly, a person walked up to Roderick and spun him in the dark.

"Oh, but you have done something wrong, Roderick." The voice was muffled and unrecognizable to him.

"What have I done? I never hurt anybody. I've never talked badly about anyone and I've never treated anyone mean. Tell me what I have done!" Roderick could see someone's shadow briefly.

"Roderick, you have succeeded in alienating everyone from me. You see me passing in the hallway, and you put on that fake smile, but it's not me you see."

"What in the heck does that mean? And how do you know me?"

"Right now, you don't need to know anything other than what I tell you. Just make sure you don't do anything foolish or else they will find your body in the lake."

Roderick squirmed in his seat to see if he could get loose. He heard footsteps, and it sounded like the person was walking away.

"Hey!" He shouted. "Don't leave me down here, please!"

A door creaked open, revealing the outline of a man that Roderick still could not recognize. "If I were you, Roderick, I would start praying." And with that, the door closed shut, and Roderick was swallowed with darkness again.

Back at Erica's house, the detectives continued to ask as many questions as they could think of. "Have you or anyone in your family received death threats?" Erica shook her head no. "Do you have any enemies?"

"Yes, the devil. And I know all of this is nothing but the devil! As far as people, I'd have to say in the past, some investigations I have been involved in were with drug dealers and other criminals, but I can't say that any of them have personally threatened me before."

"Are you doing any investigating right now?"

"I am coinvestigating a murder case, but we are in the beginning stages of the investigation. We were just assigned to it a week ago."

"How many children do you have?"

"I have three, why?"

"Because this was done in your home, and it seems as though they have been watching you. They took Roderick at the front door. This is personal. This is someone who knows you well and knows your family. If the timeline is anywhere close to what Joshua describes, that only gave them a window of about ten minutes. From the time Joshua says he and Roderick talked to the time he walked to his house. It was approximately three minutes between. That leaves seven minutes to grab Roderick, find your bedroom, knock you unconscious, and quietly take him without making a sound. Or they grabbed him coming through the door. That could explain why there was no forced entry." Detective Mutchison got up from his seat to demonstrate the scenario. "They get him to the floor next to the coffee table. That's where his tie came off and where they secured him. Then the man came and attacked you."

"Detective Mutchison, all that sounds very credible, but it just doesn't add up. Roderick has never been in trouble. He's on the honor roll and has colleges scouting him to go to their schools. In two weeks, he has to pick a college. He gets along with everyone. He's never even been in a fight. My son is a good boy."

"Ms. Vaughn, I know this is difficult. If there is anything you can think of, please call me, especially if you get a ransom note or a phone call. Here is my card."

"All right."

"We're going to leave right now. Try to relax and let me know if you can think of anyone who might be involved." Detective Mutchison and Ms. Luna got up to leave.

"Wait! To be honest, I really have no facts other than what I've seen, but my neighbor next door does very weird things at night. As a matter of fact, he doesn't come out of his house until nighttime. Sometimes, he looks at us from out of his window. When I catch him looking, he quickly closes his curtains. I really can't tell you what he looks like, other than white, about five-eight or five-ten. Like I said, it isn't much to go on, but if you could just check him out, I would appreciate that."

"Okay, thanks for that information," Detective Mutchison replied while writing in his notepad. "We will check this out, ma'am."

"You can stop calling me ma'am and start calling me Erica."

"Okay, Erica. We will check on your neighbor this evening. And again, call us if you think of anything else."

As Erica walked the detectives out the door, she saw Joshua and his parents coming down the street. As they walked up the red brick walkway to Erica's doorstep, Mrs. Dunn held out her arms to hug Erica.

"I'm so sorry this is happening to you, Erica."

"Hello, Katherine. You all come inside."

The Dunn family sat down on the sofa. "What are the police doing about this?" Mr. Dunn expressed firmly.

Erica tried hard to avoid breaking down in tears. It was too many questions for her to bear. "They just finished asking me all kinds of questions. They wanted to know if we had enemies. All I can think about is my son. I hope they aren't hurting him!"

Katherine sat closer to Erica to comfort her. "Erica, I know your faith in God is strong, and I know that whatever news you get, God is going to help you get through it. Be strong in the Lord and in the power of His might. God is here to comfort you through this. Remember, Roderick is in His hands now, and He knows what's best. These trials come to make us stronger in Christ Jesus. Stay prayerful, and God will see you through this."

Mr. Dunn prayed with Erica for her son. Mrs. Dunn was also in the prayer circle, but Joshua had disappeared, and when they were done praying, they couldn't find him anywhere in the house.

"Brad, where is Joshua? Can you go find him?" Erica asked.

Mr. Dunn went looking for Joshua and found him standing in the front yard just staring at the sky. He called Erica and Katherine over to see. "He's taking this pretty hard. This afternoon, we heard him throwing up in the bathroom. He came to me crying and asked why this was happening to his best friend."

"You know those two are more like brothers than any of the other basketball players on the team."

Erica and Katherine sat back down on the couch. "Once this situation is over and Roderick has returned home, then we will be able to praise God together."

Erica got up from the couch and stood at the front door to watch Joshua and make sure he was okay.

"Erica, we are going to go back home now. Please call us if you need anything or if you hear any news."

"All right. Thank you both for coming down."

"By the way, Erica, did you call your family?"

"Yes, they will be here tomorrow morning."

"Okay, we love you. Try to get some rest."

"I will," Erica rested her weary soul. She began to dream again. She hadn't had a dream in years.

Journal Entry: Silent Night Dream

Erica sat on the bottom of the ship in silence. The chains around her ankles brought back memories of the capturing and suffering of her people. The darkness hid her face from the others who were also chained and bound in the darkness. As the ship rocked back and forth, water seeped in and eventually rose to fill the hull where those that were bound rested their tired bones. Their bones were sore from clamoring against the chains that held them down. "Help! There's water coming down here!" she cried. Even if people heard her, they couldn't understand her tongue. "Why are we chained like caged animals? Why are we being treated like criminals? Why have they done this to us?"

No answers came, and none of the others who were bound and chained opened their mouths. It was as if they were unable to speak. The ship began to slam against the rocks like a giant was splitting the bottom of the ship wide open with its hands.

Erica and the others began to sink down into the ocean; the others vanished into the crystal-clear water, and their chains melted away—but not her. She was left behind and all alone. Gasping for air, she reached the seashore where she slept for days.

Erica was lost and confused. She had to fight to survive, and she hoped to be rescued. Several days went by with no signs of rescue.

"Why did this happen to me?" she asked herself. "I don't belong here. I'm not a slave. I was taken from my family, and now, I don't remember what they look like."

She was starved and delirious and had been walking on the island in circles. With every tree she passed, she thought she had reached a new part of the island, but then reality hit her when she would end up in a place where she had been before. She looked up to see a plane circling overhead.

~

"Mom!"

Erica screamed and woke up confused from her dream. "What's going on?"

"It's Nolan, Mom. You were having a nightmare."

"Nolan is it you?" She rubbed her eyes to see clearly.

"Mom, Detective Mutchison is here."

Erica began to cry uncontrollably. "Nolan, I don't know what to do right now. I just pray that whoever took my baby will return him!"

Nolan had never seen his mother like this before, not even when she was going through her troubles with Gary. "Mom, I know this is tough, but we have to keep it together for Roderick. You have to stop crying and come speak to the detectives."

Erica wiped the tears from her eyes and tried to collect herself. "Okay, I can do this," she said. "Nolan, tell the detectives that I'll be right down."

As Nolan left the bedroom to let the detectives know that she would soon be coming out, the doorbell rang. Nolan rushed to the door, and there stood Johnston. They hugged.

"Johnston, I'm glad you're here, man. We need you. My mom needs you."

"Where is she?"

"She just woke up. She's in the bedroom and will be down shortly. Johnston come meet Detectives Mutchison and Luna." Nolan walked Johnston over to the detectives and they shook hands.

Erica came down and walked right in Johnston's arms. Johnston's eagerness to be by Erica's side was obvious and genuine.

"Okay, I've gotten all my crying out and feeling helpless in this situation. What do we need to do to find my son?"

"Ms. Vaughn, we interviewed the limo driver Mr. Morrison. The timeframe he told us doesn't match the time Roderick's friend Joshua gave us, so we went ahead and put Mr. Morrison under surveillance. We are keeping a close watch on him. We have not yet interviewed your neighbor, but we will do that once we leave here. Right now, all we can hope for is a ransom phone call or get some evidence against Mr. Morrison, if he had anything to do with your son being kidnapped. Is there anything else you can think of regarding your attacker?"

Nolan looked up with confusion and interrupted the detective. "Attacker? What attacker?" he asked.

Erica explained to Nolan what happened to her. She hadn't told him that part of the story; she wanted to wait until he got home to tell him face to face. Erica tried to remember the details of her attacker.

She had so often taught these techniques to others.

"The man was Caucasian. He was probably in his late forties. He said, 'We have your son,' so I know there is more than one person in on this."

"If the limo driver had anything to do with this, he had to have an accomplice to help him pull this off."

"But what motive does the limo driver have against us? I've never seen the man before in my life. Not in passing or in church, and I've never investigated him in court before. Roderick is just a kid. What could he have possibly done to anyone?"

~

Roderick was being held in a dark, cold, spacious place in the morning. Then it would swelter in the afternoon. The man who kept him hostage taunted him daily and was careful to not reveal his identity.

"Your kind needs to be exterminated from the earth," the man said. "We should have wiped you out when we had the chance, but these soft liberals had to have things go their way. You're all trash, the whole lot of you."

While the man expressed vile outbursts, Roderick prayed aloud and quoted every scripture he could remember.

"God, forgive them for they know not what they do. Lord, please. Just help me get out of here."

"If it were up to me, I would have killed you already, but someone else has plans for you. Me personally, I would do you like that new girl down the block from you. She was lonely and needed a friend."

"Shut up," said Roderick. "You need Jesus." Roderick tried to recognize the voice but couldn't. He looked at the shadows all around him but was unable to see anything else.

"Roderick, the superstar athlete, and academic wiz is in the house. Where is your God, Roderick? Why hasn't He saved you yet?

Why hasn't He revealed to your family where you are? Do you want to know why, Roderick? It's because there is no God. I once believed in Him like you do, but now I don't. I got smart and freed myself from religion. I prayed to be successful. I prayed to have everything my heart desired. But do you know what, Roderick? Your

God hasn't answered any of my prayers!" The man's voice was venomous and cold. "Do you have a best friend, Roderick?" said another voice that was also unrecognizable to Roderick.

"What is it to you?"

The hidden faces looked at each other and laughed out loud. "Tell me, Roderick, what is his name?"

"Why should I tell you, his name? So, you can kidnap him too? No way! If you don't know who my best friend is, then we'll just keep it that way."

"Oh my, it sounds like someone has a soft spot for his best friend Joshua Dunn."

"If you already knew, then why did you ask me?"

"If my plans go as they are supposed to go, then you'll be able to join your friend really soon."

"You better not hurt him." Roderick, rocking, trying to get out of his restraints.

"Oh my, are you making demands? It sounds like you are to me. Well, Roderick, I wouldn't try to make demands in your position. You just might find one of your family members in a pool of blood or hung from a tree."

Roderick began to sob. With tears rolling down his face, he could think of only his mom. At this point, it was Roderick's resolve to die. He would sacrifice himself to save his family. He couldn't allow himself to be used as a pawn. His thoughts rang out loud in his ears that to die in Christ is gain. He was ready to live eternally with God. "Lord, if it is Your will, I am willing." He spoke out loud. "It doesn't matter what you do to me because as the three Hebrew boys said, even if God doesn't deliver me, I know that He is able."

~

It was now day three of the investigation. After interviewing Erica's neighbor, Detectives Mutchison and Luna decided to search the wooded area behind her creepy neighbor's house. When they visited the neighbor, Mr. Dudley Hughes, his house smelled like a sewer. The detectives learned that he had been living alone for fifteen years since his wife died. Detective Mutchison asked Mr. Hughes if they could continue the interview outside because of the unbearable smell. As the detectives interviewed Mr. Hughes, they found out some interesting facts about him. He had been arrested twice, and one time it was for assault and battery. Mr. Hughes said the love for his wife was what kept him out of trouble. They had a daughter, but because he refused to put her in school, she was sent to foster care. After that, his life started to unravel and went off the deep end.

~

It was now four days since Roderick went missing, and Detective Mutchison still had no clue where Roderick was or if he would ever be found. He began to consider Dudley Hughes a prime suspect in Roderick's case, but still there was no evidence that showed the crimes pointed to him.

"Hey! Mutchison!"

"What's up, Luna?"

"My gut is telling me that there's more to the hermit Mr. Hughes. Do you mind if we go back and search the premises again tomorrow morning?"

Mutchison looked satisfied. He always wanted to be as thorough as possible. He turned to Luna. "No, I don't mind, but what's going on in that head of yours?"

"Well, Roderick was abducted around three or so in the morning. The hermit only comes out at night, and according to the neighbors, he is sometimes seen fiddling around his house until daybreak. If nothing else, I guarantee Mr. Hughes saw something or was involved in Roderick's disappearance."

"Okay, if we want to go that route, what evidence would we be looking for? This boy vanished. All that was left was his tie."

"We are looking for anything Roderick may have dropped out of his pockets. Maybe he threw down something on purpose to leave a clue. Maybe they bound him, but he remained conscious. Maybe they told him to keep quiet or they will kill his mother. They gained access to the inside of the house somehow. We found no tracks to indicate that there was a struggle or a car in the woods. We found nothing in the limo—no blood or fibers from Roderick's clothing. We have to go back to Ms. Vaughn's and ask her what kind of jewelry Roderick might have had on."

Mutchison sat for a minute contemplating what Luna described to him. "All right let me call Ms. Vaughn to see if we can stop by to look. First thing in the morning, we will go hunting."

Luna smiled. She believed that she was going to solve this case whether Roderick was alive or dead. She believed in her abilities as a detective.

~

The next morning, the detectives asked Erica about any jewelry Roderick may have worn.

"The only thing I can think of is his watch, and he wore a tiny cross charm on his bracelet. Other than that, he wore no other jewelry."

"To update you, we want you to know we will be investigating Mr. Hughes, your neighbor. We can't discuss some of the things we have found out about him right now, but we just want you to know we will be doing a more thorough investigation after we finish here."

"But Detective Mutchison, he usually sleeps during the day."

"That's the way we want it. We want to be able to search around his house for any evidence without spooking him. If we find anything, we can call in for a warrant."

Johnston, who was there the whole time, recognized Erica was getting frustrated. He walked closer to her and said, "I want you to go take a bubble bath and try to relax. I'll take the boys to the store, and when we get back, we'll have breakfast. Then we are going to have a prayer service and discuss Roderick being taken and what our next steps should be. We all need to refocus and come together. So, go take your bath. That's an order." Erica silently agreed.

In her bedroom, she stood by her mirrored closet and loaded her gun. She placed it next to the tub as she got in. Her thoughts ran to the cold reality that Gary had never called about his son even after she left several messages. Why would a father choose anything over his own flesh and blood?

After an hour soaking in her whirlpool sauna tub, she could hear her two sons were close by talking. She quickly got out of the tub to hide the gun. Erica had been free from the bondage of sin since her last stand with Gary. Now, she felt bound because her hands were tied, and nothing in her power could change the fact that her son had been taken from her. It was a sad, humbling experience.

After putting her nine-millimeter away, she dressed and entered the kitchen, sitting at the barstool counter. Nolan and Greg were in the backyard, both on their cellphones discussing Roderick's kidnapping to their girlfriends and buddies. Johnston could see Erica was in a state of depression. She had passed the disbelief and shock stage of her son being taken, and now she began to blame herself.

"Erica, look at me. Look at me!" Johnston's voice had never sounded that demanding before. She looked over at him as though he had lost his mind, but she knew what he was about to say. After putting his fork down, he walked around to where Erica was sitting. "Do not start this blame game with yourself. Do not take on the burden of someone else's evil. Don't go down this road because you may never return. You have done right by your sons. You've done everything possible to keep them on the right track and safe. It's all in God's hands. Roderick is in God's hands, and no matter what happens, maintain your faith and sanity in Christ. You can't allow the devil to win. I love you too much to allow you to do this to yourself. I'm here with you every step of the way. Together, we are going to make sure that Nolan and Greg get through this. We will all get through this together."

Erica couldn't help but to trust Johnston; he was so passionate and convincing. She believed that no matter what happened, together they would get through this.

"I'm making your favorite for dinner later on—chicken broccoli casserole! But breakfast will be light and healthy."

"Thank you, Johnston. Thank you for everything. For always being there for me and the boys."

"You just don't get it, do you?"

"Get what? What don't I get?"

"You were supposed to be my wife, and those boys were supposed to be my sons. But God beat me to it. My love for you is stronger today than it was eighteen years ago. Reuniting with you was a dream come true for me. Like I said before, I truly wanted to see you to apologize. I prayed you were still single. After seeing you again, I fell in love with you all over again. That dream was shattered when you told me you were married to Gary. Trust me, I stayed on my knees in prayer and even sought out godly counsel to put my own desires on hold. I'm here because of my love for you and those boys. They are mine, and I would do anything for them, even if it meant dying." Tears rolled down Johnston's face. "When all of this is over, we will discuss this further. Right now, we need to focus on what's at hand and maintain normality for Nolan and Greg." Johnston wiped his tears as Greg and Nolan walked through the door. Erica placed her hand on his shoulder to show that she approved his confession.

~

The next morning, Mutchison and Luna were back on the hunt. They searched every inch around Mr. Hughes' house. As Luna began to search inside a bush next to the cellar doors, she saw something shiny.

"Hey Mutchison," Luna whispered. "I think I found something over here."

Quickly and quietly, Mutchison ran toward Luna.

"Help me push this bush back. I saw something shiny. Come on and open it up. Oh! It's only a dime."

Frustrated, Luna sighed. "Awe man," she scolded herself.

As they closed the bush, a shiny diamond earring fell to the ground.

"What might this be?"

"This looks like a woman's earring."

"But he said there hasn't been a woman around this house for fifteen years! This earring doesn't look like it's been here that long."

"Get CSI down here as soon as possible. Call the station and check to see if there have been any female murder or abduction cases reported recently. Get the names of the detectives assigned to those cases. If we get a positive ID on this earring, then I am going to ask Judge Drake for a search warrant to search the house. Get on it now." Luna and Mutchison were ecstatic to find this evidence. After receiving a phone call from the station, they found there was one female murder case assigned to FBI Agent Eriks. It would take six hours to see if the earring matched the dead girl's earring. The CSI team took pictures of the earring and sent them over to Agent Eriks to show the victim's parents. Only they would be able to identify whether the earring belonged to their daughter, Esther Greene. "Hello, Mr. and Mrs. Greene. There are some detectives investigating the kidnapping of Roderick Manning, a kid who lives just down the street from you."

"Have you found something? Have you found the monster who murdered my daughter?" Mrs. Greene said.

"I understand your anxiety, and I know you want the killer to be found, but I need you to calm down and focus. Can either of you identify the earring in this picture?"

Mrs. Greene fell to her knees. "My God, that's Esther's earring! She never took them off."

"Can you positively identify that this earring is your daughter's?"

"Yes, I can, detective. I bought them for her birthday and a moving present. The mortuary took off the other earring and replaced them since she only had one in her ear. I will get the other one from her room. I put it in her jewelry box." Mrs. Greene went upstairs to get the other earring.

Agent Eriks called Mutchison to let him know the news. He was holding up the earring as he made the call. "Detective Mutchison, call Judge Drake. We have a match to the earring found at your investigation site." Mutchison was so excited. He told the news to all the others in the department.

"Agent Eriks, what's going on?" Mrs. Greene asked.

"Well, Mr. and Mrs. Greene, another detective has been investigating an abduction case in the area—the one I told you about concerning the young man. As they were searching for a potential crime scene, they came across an earring that matched the one your daughter wore."

"Does this mean you have found her killer?" Mr. Greene asked.

"Now, I can't confirm or deny that we have a suspect. Right now, we're waiting on the judge to issue a warrant to search the house thoroughly. Although they found the earring, it was found outside his house. We can't yet say a crime was committed at this location, but we do have probable cause to bring the person in for questioning and search their home. The person in question might just confess or talk about something they saw. Anyway, I will keep you updated on the case."

The Greene's thanked Agent Eriks for his time and escorted him to the door.

~

By twelve noon the next day, the detectives were down the block with a search warrant. They walked up to Mr. Hughes' door and knocked. It took him ten minutes to come to the door because it was daylight.

"Yes, may I help you?"

"Mr. Hughes, we have a warrant to search the premises."

Mr. Hughes immediately started trying to push the door closed. "No! You can't come in here." Mr. Hughes tried to close the door, but the Georgia FBI Department rammed through and tackled him to the floor. They handcuffed him, read his Miranda rights, pulled him out of his house, and made him sit in the police unit while they searched inside the house.

Meanwhile, another team busted the lock to the cellar doors and searched diligently. They used flashlights to find the light switch. They didn't find Roderick, but they found women's underwear and clothing. They also found pictures of young girls who were tortured and maimed pictures that were pornographic and grotesque in nature.

The police found more women's clothing locked in a cabinet. They assumed the clothing belonged to the same girls. Mr. Hughes now appeared to be beyond evil, and they had enough proof to put him away for the rest of his natural life.

All of the agents for the Greene's case found what they needed to put Mr. Hughes away for life. There was still no sign of Roderick.

Detective Mutchison and Luna were waiting to go in.

"We've searched the entire house and have found nothing that could trace us to Roderick."

"Thanks, Agent Eriks. At least we got that sick bastard off the streets. Right now, I can't celebrate because I still have a seventeen-year-old kid missing."

"Well, Mutchison, I hope your case turns out better than mine."

"Can you do me a favor?"

"What can I do for you?"

"Can I interrogate him first? I just want to see if he had anything to do with the boy's disappearance or if he saw anything."

"I don't think that would be a problem. He's going down for Esther Greene's murder, and it looks like countless others even if he doesn't confess. Let me wrap this up, and you can go at him tomorrow morning. Thanks, I couldn't have done this without you. I owe you big."

"Well, it's not me you should be thanking; it's my partner Luna who cracked this one for you. She had a hunch, and we followed it."

"Thank you so much, Detective Luna! I know Esther's parents would thank you as well."

"Anytime!" Luna shook Agent Erik's hand.

Mutchison and Luna walked toward Erica's house to tell her the news. Where was Roderick? They still had no clue.

~

Roderick prayed to be found. His body was weak from being fed only bread and water once a day. He had been chained to a chair for seven days. He couldn't lie down or move because he was bound from legs to chest.

Even if he could walk, his feet and legs had been asleep for days, and they ached with pain. Roderick could only slouch enough to rest his head on the back of the chair. "God," he prayed weakly, "please just take me now. I don't know how much more of this I can take."

It was hot and humid in that empty unfamiliar place, and any water he was given came out of his sweat and soiled pants. His agony was met with Erica's anguish.

Johnston and Erica began to pray after Detective Luna and Mutchison left. After an hour and a half of praying, Erica began to speak in a language that only God could understand. She felt a peace that somehow reassured her that Roderick was still alive. She began to praise God with Johnston.

Nolan and Greg walked in the door. They were not surprised about what they witnessed. Instead, they cried at the sight of Johnston and their mother praising God through this ordeal. Nolan began to praise God along with them. Not long after, he was on his knees asking God to forgive him for not being obedient. Greg rejoiced with his brother, and they all hugged and felt comforted.

~

On the eighth day, as the morning dawn drew near, Detective Mutchison and Luna were preparing to interview Mr. Hughes. They walked down the long corridor to the interrogation room where Mr. Hughes was sitting. When the detectives came into the room, Mr. Hughes straightened up in his chair. He was short and stocky. His hair was matted to his head as if he hadn't combed it in decades.

"For the record, please state your full name."

"My name is Dudley Raymond Hughes."

"What is your current age?"

"I am forty-eight."

"Do you work for a living?"

"I kill young trashy girls for a living."

"Mr. Hughes, where is the young nigger boy you took?" It was an unexpected question and brilliant.

"That nigger boy is safe and sound…uh oh!" Detective Luna stood up to question Mr. Hughes.

"Mr. Hughes, my name is Detective Luna. We know you took him." Mr. Hughes didn't even acknowledge Detective Luna and avoided looking at her.

He looked at Detective Mutchison and said, "Would you tell this Mexican trash to stop talking to me? I only talk to pure breed white folk, and I know nothing about her is pure."

Detective Mutchison covertly waved Detective Luna off as he kept eye contact with Mr. Hughes.

"Okay, Mr. Hughes. We know you took him. All we want to know is where we can find him?"

"If you bring me a nice young girl to play with, maybe I'll tell you."

At this point, Detective Luna was seething. She wanted to be involved in the interrogation but feared she would make Mr. Hughes clam up and stop talking. She began to speak again. Detective Mutchison was about to shut her up, but he didn't want to seem obvious, so he let her continue.

"Mr. Hughes, if your wife were alive, what would she think about you doing this to your daughter?"

Instantly, Mr. Hughes began to sob with drool running down his lips. He started talking to his wife as if she were there. "Oh, Miranda. I'm sorry. I've become a mess. I know I'm no longer worthy in your eyes. For so long, I needed you to help me. They took our baby, and I found her down the street. Those Satanists down the street had our baby, but I convinced my friend Joshua to help me steal her back. He helped me get our baby back, and I rewarded him. Oh Miranda! Why did you leave me? Why did you let them take our baby girl? Why?" Then he suddenly shut down. Detective Mutchison tried to ask more questions about Roderick's whereabouts, but Mr. Hughes would not say a word. Detective Luna motioned to the guard to return the prisoner to his cell. Luna and Mutchison walked out the room to talk to Agent Eriks.

"The only thing we can go on now is that he implicated a person named Joshua in the kidnapping of Esther. He said he rewarded him. The only Joshua we know for right now is Roderick's school friend who lives down the street. The proximity of where they all live make sense, but we must make sure there are no other Joshua's in the neighborhood or at the school. We need to send a team to the school now and talk to the folks in charge. The only way we're going to find out what he meant is to bring in Joshua. Get Judge Drake on the line and explain the two cases are tied together. We need a warrant for Joshua's questioning and any Joshua at his school."

Once again, the station was buzzing. When the detectives received the warrant to bring in Joshua, they had to decide whether to take him from school or home. They decided to take Joshua from home while Detective Luna would go speak with the family about the new development.

The detectives staked out in front of Joshua's home and waited for him to arrive from school. As he walked to his front door, the police grabbed him and handcuffed him. It happened so fast that he had no time to respond or resist. As they put Joshua in the squad car, his parents ran out of the house to see what was going on.

"Mr. and Mrs. Dunn, I need to talk to you about what we have learned."

Indignant, Katherine asked, "What is your name, sir?"

"Well, ma'am, my name is Agent Eriks, and this here is Detective Mutchison." Mutchison sensed anxiety from the Dunn's and tried to speak to them calmly about their son.

"Mr. and Mrs. Dunn, I think it's best if we step into your home and discuss this."

They all walked inside of the home, and before they could even sit down, Mrs. Dunn began to cry.

"I know this may be difficult to hear," Detective Mutchison said, "but your son or a person named Joshua has been implicated in the involvement of kidnapping Esther Greene. We believe he may also be involved in Roderick's kidnapping. We arrested one of your neighbors, Mr. Hughes, for the murder of Esther Greene, the young lady who lived next door to Roderick's residence. Mr. Hughes has implicated a Joshua in helping him kidnap the young lady. The only Joshua we have on record right now is your son. This is only preliminary questioning as we must determine if there are any other viable students at their school by the name of Joshua as well. Since he's closest to this case, we must eliminate him as a suspect."

"What? Joshua wouldn't do something like that! We are God-fearing people, and we have raised our son to be the same. You must be mistaken."

"Understandably, I know this is shocking to you. Mr. Hughes stated in his confession this morning he rewarded a Joshua for helping him. Right now, I am speculating that his reward had something to do with Roderick because Mr. Hughes stated that Roderick was safe and sound, but we don't have all the details. We suspect Joshua might know where Roderick is being held."

Mr. Dunn fell silent after hearing this bit of news.

"He is eighteen, but we would like it if you would come and view the questioning. It is not customary we ask the parents, but under the circumstances, we don't know if he's going to need a lawyer. Right now, we just need the truth, and this is the only way to get it out of him."

"Detective Mutchison, I don't want to hear what he has to say. My husband will go."

Mrs. Dunn's face was filled with sorrow beyond measure. She wondered if her son was guilty. 'He had been acting strange', she thought. He was so secretive and had been disappearing quite often lately.

Mr. Dunn was in absolute shock as he passed the police car with his son sitting in the back. Joshua had no idea what was going on. As they drove to the station, Joshua kept asking questions. "Why am I being arrested? Why is my father in the other police car? Hey nigger, you hear me talking to you?"

The police officer turned toward Joshua and looked him dead in his eyes and said, "The only nigger I see in here is the one sitting in the backseat because it seems to me that you are the sick idiot."

Joshua sat back in his seat, frowning.

~

Once they arrived at the station, the black officer asked his partner to take the suspect into the interrogation room. "If you don't take him, I might give him some major injuries before he even gets in the room," he said. His partner smiled and took Joshua.

As Joshua sat in the interrogation room, he began to sweat profusely, and his legs were shaking. Detective Mutchison and Detective Luna walked into the interrogation room as Mr. Dunn watched behind the two-way mirror. Mutchison gave Joshua his Miranda Rights and went through the same procedures as he did with Mr. Hughes. "Joshua, you are here because we have received information from Mr. Hughes about your involvement with some abductions. Can you tell us what happened?"

"Well, what did he tell you? Whatever he said, he's lying."

"Tell me, Joshua. Why would Mr. Hughes single you out of all the kids on the block? Why would he implicate you? Why not Roderick or Jeffrey?"

"Roderick! Roderick couldn't help Mr. Hughes."

"Why couldn't he help Mr. Hughes?"

"Because he's black!" Joshua shouted angrily.

"Well, why not Jeffrey? He's white."

"Jeffrey is not smart. He is poor white trash and would get us all caught."

But it was Josh who wasn't smart, the detectives surmised, because he was giving them the information they needed. Luna needed to get a confession. "Roderick does everything better than you. He plays basketball better than you. He's smarter than you."

Joshua rubbed his hands together. "I know what you are trying to do, but it's not going to work."

"Joshua, what did you get on your SAT?" She looked at her notes. "Well, according to your records, you only got an 800 and Roderick scored a whopping 1950! It sure looks like Roderick is smarter than you."

"Shut up. Just shut up. Roderick isn't that smart." Joshua slammed his fist on the table.

"Why not, Joshua? He's even being scouted by colleges to play for their schools."

Joshua tried to stand up, but the chains knocked him right back down. "Shut up, I said." As the veins were starting to show in his neck and forehead. "If Roderick was so smart, then why did he allow us to kidnap him? Mr. Hughes was going to kill his mother, but I told him not to. We took him, and he still doesn't know it's me. Roderick is the stupid one. I'm not his friend. I was never his friend."

"Why did you want to hurt Roderick? Has he done anything to you? You were his best friend, and he would do anything for you. Why would you do this?"

Joshua broke down just as Mr. Hughes had. "I did it because I was supposed to have his life. My parents prayed just like Ms. Vaughn did. I prayed to the same God, and my life turned out to be nothing. My life was supposed to turn out like Roderick's. I only wanted to keep him locked up until those schools would want me instead, and then my parents would be proud of me."

"Joshua, you have to tell me where Roderick is. If you tell me, then we can let the judge know you cooperated with us. If you don't, then the judge will not look favorably on you."

Joshua laid his head down on the table and then rose with a sigh. "He's in Mr. Hughes's house."

"What do you mean? We searched Mr. Hughes's house and didn't find Roderick."

"There's a floor door underneath the dining table and carpet. That's the only way you can get to him."

Mutchison and Luna ran out of the interrogation room. Joshua stood up and tried to follow them, but he was unable to because of the chains that were holding him to the floor.

"Tell Ms. Vaughn..." he started to say something and then quieted down. "Never mind."

Joshua's father entered the interrogation room and sat across from his son in silence. Both were afraid to speak to each other.

Agent Eriks had been standing there. "I'll leave you two alone," he said.

"Son, why would you do this?" Mr. Dunn asked. "Why would you want this to be done to Roderick? He was your best friend. He's never done anything to you."

"Because I hate black people. Anyone who isn't purely white should be exterminated. The blacks are taking over everything. I couldn't even get a scholarship because they were all over Roderick. He's just a nigger who can play basketball."

"Joshua, do you even hear what you are saying? You and Roderick have been friends since the tenth grade, and now suddenly you have these feelings. Personally, I think you are lying. You're using this pure white crap to excuse what you have done. You don't hate black people; you're jealous of Roderick, and you can't handle what you are feeling. I have never shut my door to you. I have never taught you to hate others, and neither has your mother. She's going to be outraged when

I tell her."

"What do you know?" Joshua sobbed. "You don't know what goes on at school. I was the most popular kid in school until he came along. For the past two years, I've had to ride Roderick's coattail. You always tell me that I can be the best."

"But Joshua, I tell you that you can be the best in Christ, not on your own. Nothing will last if you don't have Christ in your heart. That's the difference between you and Roderick. He has kept God first and you have turned away from God."

"Well, I've prayed to your God, and He hasn't done anything for me. I had to take measures into my own hands."

"And that's why you're here chained like a caged animal because you are acting like one! Did you ever consider talking to me or your mother about how you were feeling or what you were going through?"

"No. You wouldn't have listened anyway. I found my true friend. Mr. Hughes was there for me, and he taught me everything I needed to know."

"Joshua, Mr. Hughes is a sick man. He has killed innocent young girls for pleasure. This man lost his own daughter and wife. He has taken his guilt out on everyone else for the past fifteen years— including you. Your mother and I love you and will always love you, but what you have done to that girl and to Roderick is inexcusable. You are going to have to pay for what you've done, and you will probably be paying for a long time. I'm sorry, son, but I have to go home and tell your mother the news that you won't be coming home." Mr. Dunn cried like he was a newborn baby. He walked out of the interrogation room.

~

There had been many tears shed on that day, and there would be more to come. When Detective Mutchison and Luna arrived at the Hughes home, they did not hesitate to bust down the doors. At the time they arrived, everyone next door had gone to the grocery store. They had no idea what was taking place. The detectives and two other cops moved the heavy dining table and everything else that was piled on top of it.

They pulled the rug back and found the floor door. Pulling the door back, the stench of urine and feces smoldered like an atomic bomb had just been dropped on the site. They hollered who they were and received no response. Flashlights bounced off the walls as they marched one by one down the wooden stairs. Luna called out Roderick's name, but there was no response.

Mutchison began to look for a light switch. When he found it, he switched it on, and there lay Roderick's limp body. They checked for a pulse and found nothing.

"Do you know if Ms. Vaughn and her family are home?" Detective Mutchison asked Luna.

"I'm not sure. I'll send one of the officers to see if they were home."

"Go find out," said Detective Mutchison, "and while you're up there, send the CSI team down. Also, have the coroner team come. I think we're too late."

Detective Luna sent in the CSI team to take pictures, collect any evidence, and fingerprints they could find. An hour had passed, and the coroner came in to extract the body. For Detective Mutchison, this was not a happy ending. Although the suspects had been apprehended, the frustration he felt was more bothersome than anything. He questioned why God would allow children to die like this. He pulled himself together and went outside of the house to call Erica and let her know that they found her son's body. He knew the news would be devastating. He had done these many times, but he could never get used to it. He was apprehensive but knew it had to be done.

As he got himself ready to dial the number, one of the coroner's assistants ran up the stairs.

"Get the medics in here now! The boy is alive." Detective Mutchison fell to his knees. "Thank you, God." He began to cry.

"Mutchison, get up. We must get Roderick out of this place and to the hospital—now!"

Mutchison came to himself and jumped up as fast as he could. As they were pulling Roderick up to the stairs, the medic said, "He has a faint pulse, and his breathing is shallow. We need to get him over to the hospital right away. We can't risk putting an IV in him now. We're going to put some oxygen in him."

The ambulance and the detectives were on their way to the hospital. Mutchison got on his cellphone and called Erica.

"Ms. Vaughn, this is Detective Mutchison. Get over to Georgia Memorial. We found Roderick. We are on our way to the hospital and you need to get there right away."

Erica screamed. She was in the grocery store. "They found my baby! They found Roderick!" Erica fell to her knees, right in the grocery store. Johnston, Greg, and Nolan ran to Erica.

"Wait, calm down. Where is he?" Johnston asked, confused. Erica was panting, almost hyperventilating. "He's on his way to Georgia Memorial. Detective Mutchison said we need to go now. I have to go now!"

"Give me the keys, Erica." Johnston said forcefully. "Okay! Okay!"

Johnston grabbed the keys. Everyone ran to the car and piled in. Erica praised God all the way to the hospital. It was their miracle, but God was going to get the glory.

Roderick arrived at the emergency room. He was rushed in and worked on immediately. They carefully inserted the IV. Roderick was severely dehydrated, and his bodily functions were close to failing. Most of his veins had collapsed, but they were able to find one in his foot. He had no strength and could not speak. Two days later, Roderick's eyes began to open. Erica was right by his side. Johnston, Nolan, and Greg got up from their seats as Erica began to speak to Roderick. "Baby, can you hear me? I know you can't talk right now but blink your eyes if you can hear me."

Roderick's determination was stronger than his body. He was aching from head to toe, and even his eyelids hurt when he moved them, but he was able to fight through the pain to answer, Yes. Erica pushed the button for the nurses. The nurses came rushing in.

~

It took him two weeks to fully recover and be released from the hospital.

The colleges that wanted Roderick to play for them heard about his ordeal and gave him longer to decide. Get well cards and flowers were sent from UCLA, USC, and GSU. Erica's concern was that Roderick may not fully recover to be able to play again. 'I have to leave him in God's hands for his healing.'

~

At home, everyone gathered around the dinner table to welcome Roderick home from the hospital. After their meal, they all sat in the family room to discuss what happened and to explain to Roderick who took him.

"I just want to say that we are thankful to God for your safe return. Right now, we are only going to discuss what you feel like discussing. We will let you lead this meeting. We know you have a lot of questions. We may or may not have the answers, but we will try to answer as many as we can, so fire away," Erica said.

"Well, first I want to say that I am grateful to God for allowing me to make it through this. I'm glad to be back with my family and to be alive. I know you guys have avoided telling me who did this, so I'm guessing it's someone I know. Who was it?"

Johnston decided to step in at this point. "Roderick, everyone knows who did this to you, but why, we haven't really found out yet. I know the detectives know, but they are not giving us the details. They said we would have to wait until the trial."

"I just want you to say his name."

"Honey, it was Joshua and Mr. Hughes next door. They had a voiceover tape recorder. That's why you couldn't recognize their voices. They found all kinds of crazy stuff in that house."

Roderick sighed. "I suspected it was him since I didn't see him come to the hospital. He started acting strange the last two weeks before prom. Of course, we made plans for the whole basketball team to come back to our house, but a few days earlier, Joshua insisted we drop everyone off because he said that his parents wanted him to be home by 3:00a.m., and we had to drop everyone off early. Of course, you know me, I didn't want him to get in trouble with his parents. They are stricter than you are."

"Well, I guess they weren't strict enough. I suspect it was jealousy because now that I think about it when Mr. and Mrs. Dunn came down here after you had been taken, they said that two California teams were as well scouting Joshua, and you had never mentioned anything about Joshua to us, so we figured he didn't tell you."

"I don't understand. He was like a brother to me."

Nolan jumped into the conversation. "Well, next time you choose a brother, make sure it's me or Greg—your real brothers."

"Amen to that!" Greg broke in.

They all laughed and felt grateful to have their brother back. Both Greg and Nolan jumped on Roderick's lap and began to hug him. "Aw, stop with the mushy stuff."

"Get off him! He's still recovering."

Johnston pulled Erica close to him. "Leave them alone. He needs his brothers right now. He needs for things to be normal around here. And I need you, Ms. Erica Vaughn." For the first time in eighteen years, he kissed her with passion and love. The boys stopped their horse playing and turned to see their mother and Johnston kissing.

"Well, it's about time!" one of the boys said.

"Mom, Johnston, I think I can speak for all three of us. You guys had our blessing a long time ago. We love you both." Greg said.

Johnston gave hugs all around. "When is the wedding?" Nolan asked.

"Your mother and I have a lot to discuss, but I think we will wait until this trial is over. I'm in love with your mother and have been for quite some time. But we have to send Roderick off to college. Then we'll be able to talk about us. I've waited this long, so I can continue to wait for as long as she needs me to wait."

The family concluded the night by watching movies downstairs until they fell asleep.

~

The next Sunday afternoon, Johnston flew back to California. He had to report back to his pastor since he was gone for a month. Erica returned to work that Monday morning, and the boys stayed with Roderick to watch over his recovery, since they were done with final exams.

Roderick would sometimes have nightmares about his ordeal, and when he would, Erica would lie beside him and pray until he fell asleep again.

Chapter 11

Lesson Learned...Maybe

JOHNSTON WAS BACK IN LOS ANGELES TO CHECK IN with his pastor. "Pastor, only God was a witness to our faith. Ricky had been down in that basement for eight days. The detectives even said they thought he was dead when they found him because his pulse was too faint to detect. It was both a blessing and a frightening experience to see God's miracle."

"Tell me Johnston. How do you fit into all of this?"

"What do you mean?"

"There is a purpose and a reason for everything. God wanted you to witness Roderick's journey. What have you learned, and how has this experience strengthened your faith?"

"To be honest, just being there for Erica, Nolan, and Greg during all of this really has confirmed how important family is to me. But I think most of all, even if Roderick had not lived through this, we would have come out just as strong. It brought us to the trueness of God's power and mercy, and it brought us to the reality that we are not in control. Yes, we had to choose to have faith and believe, but we had no control over that madman taking Roderick nor did we have any control over Joshua telling the detectives where he was. What if Joshua hadn't revealed where Roderick was? He was right next door, and we had no clue how to find him. We had to rely on God's strength. We prayed fervently for his return, but in the end, we gave it over to God.

We were willing to accept whatever God's will was for his life. We had to stand on God's word and His love for us and believe in His power no matter the outcome."

"Wow, I know that young man has a testimony to share. Tell me, what's next?"

"We're just waiting for the trial. The older man's defense team is trying to use the insanity plea, but this is a man who has been killing young girls for the past ten years or more. We don't know how long the trial will last. You know me, I don't plan to shuck my responsibilities, but when the trial comes, I would like to be there for the family."

"Oh! I would never ask you to stay away from your future family." The pastor smiled. At first, Johnston looked stunned at his pastor, but then he felt relieved.

"Yes, pastor, I have to admit that I am in love with that woman. I love her so much. I almost called you and told you I wasn't coming back."

"I'm sure glad you didn't. Not that I am being selfish or anything, but if you ever leave us, we will certainly want to send you off well."

"I know. Like I said, I would never leave you hanging. I have prayed about her, and I know she is meant to be my wife, but I have to wait on God for the right time. My only concern is how I'm going to get her back down here to California. When she left, she vowed to never come back. Of course, she has come to visit but never to stay."

"Johnston, have you ever considered moving out there?"

"No, not really. I have my life and ministry here, and God has not said otherwise."

"By the way, I received a letter from the president of the minister's convention, and with that letter came high accolades for the message you gave. I heard it was on fire in that place."

"All glory belongs to God. Trust me, I stepped up to that podium, and when I finished, I had no idea what was said or how I said it. The spirit of the Lord took over. I wish you could have witnessed it. I mean, thousands of men gathered on one accord."

"Well, if I had gone, you wouldn't have been able to preach. Pastor Hollygrove would like you to go down to his church in August to preach for their men's day."

"I would love to. This time you need to come with me."

"Of course, I will. The women do well without us anyway. My wife can be over the service."

"How is Lucille? I haven't seen her since I've been back."

"She is doing great. She has been helping with our daughter's wedding plans."

Johnston chuckled. "Wow, Robert finally got up the nerve to propose. I remember when he came to me to ask about how to propose and get your consent. That was about a year ago. He was sweating bullets then. How did he do?"

"He was still sweating bullets, but he made it through. He invited us and his parents out to his home and proposed to my daughter there."

"Awesome. He's a good guy. I'm glad Jacqueline found someone good. They're getting harder and harder to find, but there are two boys I know for sure that some women would like to get their hands on. Greg and Roderick are such respectable, God-fearing young men. Nolan, the eldest, is engaged, and while we were going through this ordeal, he totally surrendered and asked God to forgive him for his sins. I tell you, that type of experience was life-changing for everyone involved. The father of the boy who helped kidnap Roderick is the pastor of one of the largest churches in Atlanta. Joshua's parents were absolutely devastated, but from what I heard, they are not posting bail for him. In a week, Roderick will decide which college he wants to attend. He's been offered full scholarships to some of the colleges to play the starting position on their varsity teams."

"I can only imagine what that young man has been through," said Johnston's pastor. "I pray it doesn't happen to anyone again."

"Amen to that."

~

It was a couple of weeks after Roderick's recovery that Johnston returned to Atlanta. This was graduation season, and the valedictorian had Roderick speak in her place.

Roderick's graduation speech:

"God is a jealous God, and we cannot put anyone before Him, not even those whom we love to death and would die for. We have to turn our loved ones over to God and allow them to go through their own trials. They must make their own mistakes and learn from their own experiences—we can't do that for them. It's important for people to learn on their own because what we learn is not just for ourselves. We learn to help others see the glory of God in every situation—good, bad, or indifferent. This is what my mom said to me after my experience was over. She said that we are not our own, but we were bought with a price, and that price could be whatever God allows. God grants us the serenity when we make the choice to accept His will over our own. My life was spared because God heard my cry. He didn't hold my fear against me, but he allowed me to channel it through prayer and praise. I stand before you today as a person who is grateful, appreciative, and humbled by my experience. I stand before you today as a stronger believer in God and a faith walker. I say today that our parents can't save us, our teachers can't save us, and neither can our friends save us. We can only be saved through the blood of Jesus Christ. I could have had the same fate as Esther Greene, another young victim who unfortunately lost her life. It wasn't that I was a better person than Esther, but God had mercy on me so I could stand here and tell you that you can make it in God. Esther is not with us, but she would want us to fight for life, freedom, and justice. We have to fight for the Esther Greene's of this world and pray for the Joshua's everywhere. I assure you today one way or another, we will all be judged according to what is in our hearts, not the things we've accomplished or the mistakes we made. What does it profit a man to gain the whole world and lose his soul? We can't afford to lose our souls to stuff.

We can't lose our souls for fancy cars and big houses. It's okay to have those things, but we should be so careful not to not put those things before God. Stand up and make something out of our lives and make every day count. We can't take life for granted. We can't expect the best return for our troubles if we are not allowing God to rule our hearts, minds, and souls. Let's remember Esther and make her life count. We must be open for God to use us for His glory, not our own. We can make a difference where we are if we just believe in God and believe in ourselves.

In my closing, I was going to wait to make my announcement tomorrow, but I decided to not make my family, my team, and my class- mates wait any longer. The school I've chosen to attend is UCLA."

The class cheered and screamed at the top of their lungs. From the faculty to the parents, there wasn't a dry eye in the building. "Whoop, whoop, whoop!" was all to be heard for five minutes straight. Roderick walked off the stage and hugged his mother.

"I somewhat expected this, but I wish you would have told me," Erica said.

Roderick hugged her tightly. "I have to go where God is sending me. Trust me when I say I have received my confirmation."

"Well, all right then."

"Thanks for everything, Mom."

Erica didn't let go of her son right away. "I love you baby." Erica was not happy with Roderick's decision to go back to California, but she thought of her son's speech and accepted the fact that she had to allow him to go through his own trials.

She was still bothered that Gary, Roderick's biological father who lived in California, still had not called through all that occurred. "Roderick," Erica warned her son. "I just want you to understand that it goes both ways. Children cannot save their parents. Until your father accepts Christ, he will not look out for your best interests."

"Mom don't worry. Gary will always be my father, but I am not the naïve little boy I used to be. Johnston has been more of a father to me than Gary's ever been. I continue to pray for my dad's salvation, but I know he must be open and want that for himself. Anyway, can we talk about something else? Better yet, let's get back to the celebration."

~

The next week, Erica and the boys were back in California. A part of her missed being there because this was where she grew up and spent most of her life, but it wasn't long before she remembered why she left. They went to church on Sunday morning, and Johnston brought the word.

"I am excited to have in our midst today a family that has gone through some tragic and miraculous blessings through the past three months. Roderick, the young man that went through an unimaginable ordeal, will be sharing his testimony this evening, so I encourage all of you to come back tonight and worship the Lord with us. As I close, I just want to remind you that God has a purpose, a time, and a solution for everything we go through. It is not without prayer and seeking God that I was able to recently receive confirmation through pastor, a great man of God, about a decision I had to make. As all of you know and have known for many years, when I advise or counsel others, I am going to follow that counsel myself. I would like to ask Erica to join me up here in the pulpit. I need Roderick to come up here as well. I am doing things decently and in order. I asked pastor if I could do this, and he said yes."

Both Erica and Roderick walked up to the pulpit.

"The pastor of this fine ministry and I want to present to you and your family this award for outstanding courage and faith in our God and for standing up and speaking out for believers and encouraging others to seek Jesus as their Savior."

The congregation clapped for joy and praised God. Afterward, the pastor handed Roderick the plaque, and Johnston began to speak. "And you, Ms. Vaughn, I have loved you since the first day we met. I know we made mistakes in the past, but we have asked God to forgive us and made it right. Then we met each other again, and this time I am truly in love with you. This time in my life, I can say that God has blessed our friendship and has caused me to realize I am complete, but I want to become one with you." Johnston got down on one knee. "I am asking you to marry me, Ms. Erica Vaughn."

Cheers rang through the church—even the fan club that had once given Erica a hard time applauded. No one could hear Erica's response, but everyone in the congregation knew she accepted Johnston's proposal because she shook her head up and down. Johnston slipped the ring on her finger, and they briefly kissed. As the cheers continued, Johnston motioned for his pastor to take over.

Together, they walked down from the pulpit as a family and sat in the audience.

~

"Man, that was dope!" Roderick said on their way home. "I do have a confession to make. I figured Johnston would propose to you. With you guys getting married, I feel even better about going to school in California."

"So, had Johnston not proposed, you would have picked GSU?"

"Not necessarily. I just feel better about leaving home now. I mean, I would probably live on campus even if I were going to GSU. But with you two together, I feel more comfortable with the decision I made."

"Well, I am glad we were able to help. You have our support wherever you go, so you don't have to worry about me."

Johnston drove through a drive-thru to get a bite to eat. "Were you surprised?" he asked Erica.

"Yes! It was amazing. You got me good with that plaque."

"I had to get you up there somehow. But that plaque was really from the pastor and first lady."

"Thank you for making it special."

"You are welcome, my love."

"Oh god! Here we go with the mushy stuff," said Roderick.

Chapter 12

Moving On

A MONTH HAD PASSED, and the prosecutor for Mr. Hughes would also be prosecuting Joshua. The trial for the other ten girls whom Mr. Hughes had murdered would begin as well. Although Mr. Hughes faced several counts of kidnapping, rape, and murder, both Joshua and Mr. Hughes would be tried for Esther Greene and
Roderick.

As the trial began, the news media scrambled to follow up with Roderick's story. At night, they would camp out in front of the house and would follow them to the courthouse each day they went. Erica was grateful to be an employee there because the family could retreat to her office to get away from the media.

The defense for Joshua and Mr. Hughes was limited to family and very few other witnesses. The trial progressed until the defense finally rested their case.

"We will adjourn right now and will reconvene on Monday the seventeenth, with the prosecution presenting its case against the defendants at 9:00 a.m." The gavel hit the mahogany pad. "All rise. The Honorable Judge Drake is leaving the bench."

~

Erica and her family arrived at home and went through their regular routine. On Saturday morning, Johnston cooked breakfast for everyone, and afterwards the boys went off to hang out. Nolan and Greg would have to leave for school on Sunday, but for now they just enjoyed each other's company. Johnston and Erica were left to themselves.

"I have been avoiding this conversation with you, but I think it's time for us to discuss it since this trial seems to be nearly over. Before I go back to California, I need to know if I will be moving out here with you or if you'll be moving to California with me."

"I've been trying to avoid this conversation just like you have. I have prayed and prayed, and I really don't know what to do. I think about you and the ministry you have at your church. You could take over one day, and I wouldn't want you to miss that opportunity. On the other hand, I have a career here and a new life that God has provided. There is no doubt God sent me here, but I also know everything is for a season. I just really don't know what to do."

"Taking over a church is not a concern for me. God has opened so many doors for me to minister, and if He really wants me to be over a congregation, then He will make it happen no matter where I am. My concern is knowing whether our happiness is here or in California. We have to decide what we're going to do, and both of us will have to be comfortable with that decision."

"Well, let's look at the pros and cons of both choices. We can sell either one of the houses or rent it out. Either way it goes, I'm still going to have one or two of my children out of state."

Johnston walked over to Erica and caressed her, holding her close. "Why don't we just table this for now? Later, we'll come up with a plan and see where God leads us."

"I know another subject we need to discuss as well."

Johnston stepped back from Erica. "What is it?"

"Children. You don't have any of your own."

"Honey, we are free from diapers, childcare, and sickness. Nolan, Greg, and Roderick are mine. I have spent many years developing a relationship with them. We are not spring chickens and having my own children does not define who I am as a man. If it came down to it, we could adopt a baby, just like you did with Nolan, but other than that, I don't have to have a child."

"I am so glad you said that because I'm too old!" They both laughed with sincerity.

"But you know Sarah had a child in her old age," said Johnston jokingly.

Erica stopped laughing. "What you talkin' bout, Johnston?" The laughing commenced.

~

After fourteen weeks of testimonies going forth from the prosecution, Joshua and Mr. Hughes were finally given the verdicts they deserved. The sentencing would commence in one month.

~

Joshua requested to speak on his own behalf. "I don't regret anything I did. I have no remorse because given the chance again, I'd kill him for sure!"

The judge did not want to hear anymore and instructed Joshua to sit down. It was unfortunate to see Joshua's parents in the corner of the courtroom crying. Both Mr. Hughes and Joshua were instructed to stand to hear their sentencing.

Joshua would spend one year in jail at the Maximum-Security Detention Center for Youth, and once he was nineteen, he would spend the next seventy-five years in a Georgia State Prison without the possibility of parole.

Mr. Hughes was sentenced to twenty years for kidnapping and attempted murder, and after the murder trial was over for the ten young ladies, he would have two consecutive life sentences without the possibility of parole.

Mr. Hughes's life had become meaningless after his wife died. He couldn't find his way back to reality. His life exemplified a man who was lost, like Judas Iscariot. His truth was found in murdering young, innocent girls.

"I'm just glad it's over," Roderick said. "I have to start school in six weeks."

"Babe, what do you want to do now?" Erica asked Johnston.

"Roderick, did you hear that? She called me babe. She used to call me babe when we first got together. It sounds much sweeter now from those sanctified lips."

"Oh, stop! You are a mess."

Johnston pulled her close and whispered in her ear. "I love you very much, soon-to-be Mrs. Matthews."

"I love you too. Thank you for loving me for me. I thank you for just being here with me."

"Oh! You two need to get married already," Roderick interrupted. "When is the big day?"

"To be honest, we don't know yet. We have to decide where we're going to live. When I get back next week, we should have an answer for everyone."

"That's cool. Whatever you decide, just let me know ahead of time. I would like to come to the wedding."

"You know good and well you will be available, so stop playing around. Besides, I don't know if I want to plan a big wedding." Erica said this to bait Johnston into finding out what he really wanted.

"Once again, your mother and I have a lot to discuss, but we will let God lead and direct our paths in this matter."

"No doubt," Roderick expressed his approval.

God's faithfulness to them was more than they could ever imagine.

~

Pastor Morgan stood to witness Johnston and Erica's vows being read. Johnston was first. "The Bible says in 1 John 4:17–18 that *'here in is our love made perfect, that we may have boldness on the day of judgment…there is no fear in love, but perfect love casteth out fear.'* Through God, I have found that perfect love in you, and I am in love with you, Erica Vaughn."

Johnston and Erica turned toward Pastor Morgan.

"Erica, you may now say your vows," Pastor Morgan said softly.

"First John 1:4–5 also says, *'He that saith I know Him and keepeth not his commandments is a liar and the truth is not in him. But whoso keepeth his word, in him verily is the love of God perfected: hereby we know that we are in Him.'* I say this because you know them by their fruit.' You have been a great example to me and have shown me how two people can really love each other if they keep God first. I love you because you are my best friend. I am in love with you because you keep God's commandments and have been a true example to our sons."

They each took turns to put on the rings, and then Pastor Morgan closed the ceremony.

"I now pronounce you husband and wife. You may kiss your bride, Johnston."

They did not hold back from expressing their love for each other.

"I now introduce to you Mr. and Mrs. Johnston Matthews."

Tears of joy ran down Erica's face as they walked out of the church doors. Some of the women who ushered weren't so happy, but they couldn't do anything to stop the wedding.

At the reception, which was next door, Johnston and Erica danced to their wedding song and then went around to greet their guests.

~

Fifteen hours later, they were on their way to a honeymoon in Italy, and they arrived as the sun was rising over the horizon.

"This view is so beautiful," Erica said.

Johnston looked at her staring at the sun. "You are beautiful."

"Thank you, kind sir. Thank you for this fairytale, at least for a few weeks."

"You are more than deserving of a vacation, honeymoon, or whatever you want to call this. How long has it been since you've been out of the country?"

"A year or two before I adopted Nolan. Wow! Twenty-six years. I do deserve a vacation, don't I? A group of us went to the Bahamas."

"Yes, you do, and to give you more good news, I am selling the house and moving to Atlanta."

Erica turned to look Johnston in the face. "What? That's not what we discussed."

"I know, honey, but let me explain. Remember a year ago when I spoke at Pastor Hollygrove's church?"

"Yes, I remember that very clearly."

"Well, it turns out Pastor Hollygrove was actually interviewing me. He wants me to replace him next year. I wanted to discuss this with you before I gave him my answer because it's a big step for you too. You would be the first lady of True Vine Ministries."

"You know I will support you in whatever decision you make when it comes to ministry. God is leading you in this direction, so you have to be obedient to His call."

"He wants to introduce me to the congregation next month. I told him I needed some time to sell the house and move everything to Atlanta."

"I am so happy for you. I know Pastor Morgan has prepared you well. Well, since that decision has been made, what shall we see first?"

"Let me just make it plain. We have three weeks to see a lot of sites. It has been thirteen years since I was in a committed relationship. I plan on making up for lost time, woman."

It was a hysterically funny moment, and all Erica could do was laugh until she cried. Her sides and stomach were cramping, and she could barely move or breathe. Johnston stood there and chuckled. He loved to make Erica laugh, but he was dead serious. Johnston was a natural comedian who could tell a story that would keep a crowd entertained. To Erica, he was a charismatic, loving, romantic, strong, no-nonsense, and compassionate man. She loved him for these reasons, but most of all she loved him because he was a true man of God. Erica was no fool. She knew God had brought them together again the right way. She knew how to please her man. She laid on the bed to rest her body. She called Johnston over to her side. He kissed her on her cheek.

"I just want you to know you can ravish my body anytime you want."

He lied next to her. "Thank you for the invitation, babe."

They stayed in the Excelsior Palace, a five-star hotel in the city of Liguria, Italy. The Italian Riviera was at their beck and call. The mountains that surrounded them brought tranquility as the warm blue-green waters of the Mediterranean mesmerized them and helped them fall in love with each other all over again. They had not been to a more beautiful place than the Riviera di Ponente. All the sites were breathtaking. Johnston chose this place because his parents had once gone. "I never told you the story about my parents coming here."

She turned to him and grabbed his hand while they were still in bed. "No, you didn't."

"When I was fourteen, my father cheated on my mother with a woman at his job. He was about to leave my mother for this woman, and of course, my mother had no clue. They had only been seeing each other for a couple of months. Shortly after, my older brother Peter became ill. He was in the hospital for a month because he had to get a blood transfusion to treat an infection he got from stepping on a rusty nail. They tried antibiotics, but it didn't work. Out of guilt, my father tried to break off the affair with the other woman. She was not happy about it and threatened to tell my mother. My father knew he had to tell my mom first, and he did a week before my brother got out of the hospital."

"Wow," said Erica. "I would have never guessed your father cheated on your mother. They seemed to be so peaceful with each other, especially at the dinner we had with them after that church service. They seemed so in love with each other."

Johnston continued. "You've seen my mother—petite, a statue of beauty. She tried to please my father in every way without losing who she was in the process. Well, this same woman lost it that day my dad told her about his affair. My mom broke everything she could in that house. I've only seen her like that one other time when they let my uncle stay with us for a while and found out he was a child molester. I was not there when all of this occurred, but when I got home, the wreckage was just amazing. I asked my dad what was going on. My mother stepped out of the kitchen and told my father, 'You better tell him the truth. The whole truth, so help you God.' I mean, the look on my mother's face was scary. Talk about the bride of chucky and Sophia from The Color Purple all mixed in one. My mother got the keys to the car and headed out the door. I'm telling you, that door almost broke. My dad sat me down and told me everything, and to be honest with you, I wasn't shocked or disappointed at what he had done. I guess that's why I was stupid when I got married the first time."

"So how did they get back together?"

"It was my father's doing. My mother stayed at my grand- mother's for a week. My father cleaned up the house. On the day my brother got out of the hospital, he had one of his buddies take us over to the hospital. We beat my mom there. We were in my brother's hospital room when my mother walked in. As soon as he saw her, he started crying. My mom walked over to him and hugged him in silence. My brother was looking at me as though he wanted to ask me what was going on. I bent down to the level of his ear and told him we would talk about it later. That next Sunday, my dad gave his life to the Lord. Remember, I tried that with my ex-wife, and it didn't work, but now I know why."

Erica laid her head on Johnston's chest. "Why, Mr. Matthews?"

"Because she wasn't you." Erica was clay in his hands. "Anyway, about three months later, my mom and dad renewed their vows and came to this very place for their second honeymoon."

Erica looked at him and kissed him passionately. "I love to hear your stories."

"Well, Mrs. Novelist, you tell stories well yourself. Tell me, why have you stopped writing?"

Erica felt uncomfortable answering that question. She sighed because she didn't want to answer him.

"Oh no, you are not going to shut down on me now. We promised each other we would talk about everything."

"Johnston, I know but—"

"There is no 'but.' We are here together to help each other in whatever struggles we are going through. You can't expect solutions to come when you're not willing to be open. I know you love and trust me. If a woman comes after me, I'm going to tell you about every one of them because you know the man you have is fine. Alleluia!"

"Johnston, you have lost your mind."

"I've lost my mind over you, and I'm here for you."

"Johnston, I don't know if I have the desire to write anymore. To be honest, when I was writing before, it was a release for me. When I wrote those two books, it was the only thing I could do to release my anger and frustration. Even after I finished them, I still felt empty.

Once I really committed my life to the Lord, I didn't feel that urge to write anymore. I was praying and talking to God instead of writing my feelings away. I didn't need the pen to release the pain, guilt, and shame I felt all those years."

"I know about looking at your sin on paper. You know, at first, I was mad when I read about what our relationship had done to you. Part of me felt like I was being exposed too."

"Back then, that was the only way to tell on myself and hide the truth about myself at the same time. I was scared to be judged. Right now, I don't even know what I should write about. Don't get me wrong, I love writing, but I just don't have anything to write about."

"I'll tell you what. When we get back home, we will pray about it together because I know you would rather be writing than training for the court."

"You are right about that. I do like my job though, but I could let it go."

"Hold on now. I don't need a housewife. I will support you in whatever you decide to do, but don't think I want you at home all day."

"Wait a minute, mister. Don't get it twisted. You may be my husband and the head of our household, but when there is a major decision to be made, we will make it together. You got that?"

"Yes, ma'am. I love a woman who knows how to keep her man in check."

"All right don't let me have to become Sophia up in here." They both laughed and embraced.

Their final week in Italy was the most memorable of all. They saw paintings from Monet to Bolanski. These were twentieth century masterpieces from the Musee d'art Moderne de Saint-Etienne. Johnston's favorite exhibit was the Italy in Motion—one hundred years of art and vintage motorcycles. They were also able to enjoy an opera at the Teatro Massimo Bellini (Catania). They saw Spartacus.

They walked around Italy and dreaded the day they'd have to return home. Their bodies were refreshed from exploring Sorrento on the tour of Italy.

Fifteen hours later, they were back in Atlanta to face the world and their lives together. Gauging the prospects of being a pastor's wife, Erica thought about Joshua's mom, Katherine. Though it would be awkward, Erica decided to visit Katherine to see how things were. Katherine's husband, Brad, answered the door.

"Hi Erica. How's everything?" His smile was wide, but he couldn't hide his pain.

"Hi Brad. I came to see Katherine."

"Come on in." Erica walked into the house. "Unfortunately, she's not doing so well. She had to be hospitalized. During the trial, she became deeply depressed and had a nervous breakdown. She's been in and out of Georgia's State Mental Institution for a while now. She just couldn't handle the shame Joshua brought upon our family. She won't even speak to me. Right now, all I can do is pray."

Erica hugged Brad to reassure him she held nothing against him or his family.

"Brad, I am so sorry to hear this. Why didn't you call me?"

"Erica, Katherine was so ashamed. I couldn't even mention your name without her crying. Every time I tried to get her to return your phone calls, she would just break down and cry. I really couldn't call or come down to see you because I had to look after her. We would go to church, and as soon as we walked through the doors, she would break down and cry. Several times I had to leave church early to take her home. Part of me just wanted to shake her out of it, but now I doubt whether she believed God could bring us through all of this. How could you put so much faith in a child or any other human being for that matter? She was absolutely devastated by what he did, and now only God can help her. She was so paranoid that I had to admit her to the hospital. It's heartbreaking really, but the Lord gives, and the Lord takes away."

"Brad just remember Job. God allowed him to go through that test because he knew Job's heart. Job lost everything, but it was for a purpose. God restored him and gave him children and wealth when he lost everything. Trials come to make you stronger. It wasn't just my family that went through, but it was your family and the Greene family.

All those families who are still looking for their loved ones without any resolution. God can and will restore us all if we just keep our trust in Him. I am not in the position to say whether God will restore Katherine, but I trust that God knows what's best. He doesn't make mistakes. Your purpose in this was to grow in Him with or without Katherine, and He is going to do great and marvelous things in your life. The next time you go to see your wife, please let me know so I can give you a tape for her. Also, ask her if she'd be all right with me coming to visit her."

"I plan to see her next week. If she is coherent and speaking, then I will ask her and let you know what she says."

"Thank you, Brad." Erica hugged him and then left for home.

As she walked home, she thought about how grateful she was for her life. She didn't have to worry about Johnston cheating on her or not supporting her in her endeavors. Although she had been in love with Gary once, loving Johnston was different. She knew she didn't have to pray in secret. She could praise God in her home and in the open because Johnston did it too. They accepted each other. Of course, they knew that it wouldn't always be easy; the enemy would try his best to thwart what God had done for them, but they were a power couple.

~

Within three and a half months, the house was sold in Cali. As they began to go through all of Johnston's personal items and his parents' items, they considered what they would keep, sell, give away, or just get rid of. It was obvious to Erica that there would have to be some compromising and serious negotiating.

"Honey, we can't throw that away. I've had that chair for twenty-years."

"Johnston, it looks like you have sat in it for fifty years! Look, if we keep all this stuff, we will have to either buy a bigger house or add on to the one we have. And if that doesn't do it for you, remember when you helped us move to Georgia? It was painless, wasn't it?" Erica stood there with her hands on her hips.

"Yes, dear."

"We want this to be as painless as possible. We will go through your parents' belongings first, and then we will go through yours. I understand the sentimental value of what your parents left behind and the things you have collected over the years but let go of some things. You can keep your sports memorabilia and some of your parents' things, but you can't take everything. No furniture, and especially not that chair. We have five bedrooms. We will each have an office, and you will have a game room, so when you invite the men or the kids to the house, then you can use the sports room as a meeting room as well. How does that sound?"

"You're right. Since I get a game room, I will deal with the compromise."

"See how painless that was? And I didn't have to use this body to get my way either."

Johnston laughed. "You know that's not right."

~

Georgia had become their home. Saint Julian's Place in the city of Conyers was where they made their living space, and in a few months, their church, True Vine Ministries, would be their second home.

'What is it like to be a first lady?' Erica thought. Really, what will be expected of me? No matter what, she was determined to be a first lady who stayed true to herself.

Chapter 13

Manning, Who Art Thou?

SOPHMORE YEAR AT UCLA WAS AN EXCITING TIME for Roderick. This year, his team would go to the NCAA Championships with Roderick being the star player. He stayed humble and honest about his ability to play the game, and it was never a surprise to anyone when he gave God the credit for his accomplishments. He was determined to succeed, and he indeed succeeded on the basketball court as well as in his studies.

Studying was second nature to Roderick, but girls were not. He would often call Johnston for advice. There was one girl, April, who caught his eye and his heart. April was a Christian girl studying law. She was beautiful. Her smile was intoxicating to him, and at the same time she had an innocent look. She had dark hair, and her skin was a caramel complexion with faded freckles on her cheeks and arms that made her beauty stand out. She moved gracefully and was shaped like a dancer.

When Roderick spoke to his parents, he would send pictures of him and April together. Erica's only words to him were to be careful and keep his focus on God. She knew that if Roderick took his focus off of God, her past sin, which was fornication, would probably become his.

"Johnston, what do you think of this April?"

Johnston looked up at Erica as he lay on a couch reading a book. "I can't say much about her because we haven't met her yet. But from what Roderick tells me, she leads a prayer group and is the president over the Christian club they belong to."

Erica sat next to Johnston. "I don't know, Johnston. I don't want Roderick to get caught up like we did."

Johnston realized his reading would have to pause for this conversation. He set his book on the table and sat up to give his full attention to his wife. "Erica, we have taught him about what it means to abstain, but the reality is that he has no supervision in California. His brother is married and lives three hundred miles away. God will help Roderick, but if he chooses to do stupid things anyway, then he will have to pay the consequences just like we did. Every person that commits fornication will pay a price. All we can do is pray."

"They are supposed to come down to visit for summer break. I'll see about her then."

"Just make sure you are not too harsh."

"What do you mean?"

"What I mean is that you are afraid Roderick will follow in our footsteps, and that no girl is good enough for him unless you pick her."

"That's not true. Why would you think that?"

"Because I heard one of your prayers, and I'm pretty sure the Holy Spirit slapped you in the face for that one. About five months ago, I heard you pray that Roderick would not find a girlfriend until he finished college."

"Man, you have lost your mind. That's why you should never eavesdrop on someone's prayer. I finished my prayer and was talking to Yolanda on the phone, you dope."

"Oh! I am so sorry. I repent. I repent for my ways, Lord."

"Yeah, you better get up there on that altar Sunday before you preach."

"Why do you have to be so harsh?"

"You are using that word too many times, Johnston Matthews. I'm going to have to break something to show you harsh."

"See, that is what I'm talking about right there. Come here, baby. I can take that har…I can bring that tension down."

"You are lucky I love you, or I'd have to tell God on you because you know God don't like ugly."

Johnston grabbed her again. "Oh! Baby, you know I'm just fooling with you."

~

Erica's mother, Mrs. Geraldine Vaughn, lived a life she had always admired. Her mother was a taskmaster and was always so generous. Both of her parents were no strangers to the gospel of Jesus Christ, and they taught her as well as Erica's other siblings about the Word of God and what it really meant to pick up the cross and follow Jesus. She knew her parents weren't always saved.

Maggie, the youngest of the sisters, had a gift every woman around her was afraid of. When they were growing up, Maggie used to say she dreamed about fish all the time. It wasn't until her teenaged years that everyone realized her gift of revealing pregnancies. This made all the girls in the house afraid of her.

I think that's why none of us ever had sex before the age of eighteen, Erica thought. Even after eighteen, we still had to be careful if we were living in Mama's house. This was Maggie's gift, but it was also a curse to some. One day, it would cause strife within the Vaughn home. Three girls, Jennifer, Erica, and Maggie, and one brother, Ashton, filled the Vaughn residence. Jennifer was the oldest at nineteen, Ashton was eighteen, Erica was sixteen, and Maggie was fifteen.

Early one morning, Maggie rose and said she had dreamed about fish. It wasn't until that afternoon she confronted Erica about her dream.

"What do you mean, someone is going to have a baby?" Erica screamed.

"Erica, someone is pregnant, and that someone is Jennifer." "Are you sure?"

"I am absolutely sure, and I'm scared to say anything because in my dream it shows she loses the baby. If I say something, she might do something drastic. See, Erica, I don't know how she's going to lose the baby or when."

Erica contemplated what would happen if her parents found out. "Well, I think you should tell her and let her make her own decision, if she's pregnant."

"Are you saying you don't believe what I'm telling you?"

Erica was getting frustrated with her sister. "No, Maggie. It's not that I don't believe you, but maybe if you say something now, it might prevent her from getting pregnant."

"Erica, it doesn't work that way. When I have dreams, the person is already pregnant. This time, it even scared me because I saw Jennifer's face. Usually, I don't see the person's face. I just get a sense that it's someone I know."

"Well, you are going to have to say something to her. I already know how she's going to react. She will get angry and try to kill you, but she will get over it. If she tries to do anything, then we will have to get Mom involved."

Maggie looked pitiful. "Maybe you can tell her for me, Erica?"

"Maggie, if you want me to do that, I will, but she will know it's coming from you."

"I don't mind that part. I just don't want to be around for the initial shock of it all."

"Okay, I will talk to her about it when she comes home from school. You better be right about this one, though, Maggie."

The day ran smoothly. The weather was breezy and normal for that season. The California sunshine didn't last long, and an explosion was about to happen in the Vaughn household. The sky was overcast, and rain and thunderstorms brewed.

Erica walked in the room and stared into Jennifer's big beautiful brown eyes. Her eyes stretched even wider at the stance that was shown by Erica's body language. "She says it's you." Judging by the way Jennifer screamed at the top of her lungs, someone would have thought she had been stabbed. Tears rolled down Jennifer's face, and her sisters desperately tried to shut her up and calm her down before their mother heard the noise. But it was too late. "What in God's name is going on in here?" Erica crouched in the corner to avoid the wrath that was to come. It wouldn't have been so bad if just two days before, Jennifer hadn't lied to her mother about being a virgin. She even dared her mother to take her to the doctor to get checked. Of course, that convinced Mrs. Vaugh that she was telling the truth, and since Jennifer never mentioned anything about boys, the assumption was that she was not having sex.

As Jennifer grew up, it seemed that she and her mother constantly argued because they were so much alike. Their voices were the same, they both had quick tempers, and they looked like they could have been sisters instead of mother and daughter. They were both strong-willed and courageous in a lot of ways, but Mrs. Vaughn could not accept any of her daughters having children before they were married and ready to be mothers. "If nothing else, I taught you girls how to keep your legs closed and your focus on your studies. You know what happens when you lay down and don't protect yourself. What were you thinking? Did you consider the consequences? Since you were eleven, your father and I told you that we would not be taking care of any children. If you are old enough to lie down and get pregnant, you are old enough to get out on your own and take care of that child yourself. I will give you three months to get a job. Your father and I will help you get a place, but you are on your own after that. I still love you and will be there for you when you need us. But you have to go!" Jennifer shrugged at the fact she would have to leave home.

Instead of waiting three months, she left that night to be with a man ten years her senior. She thought that he would take care of her, but she was wrong. It hadn't been a week before her father and mother received a phone call from the hospital stating Jennifer had lost the baby. The father of the baby had beaten and kicked her down the stairs. He disappeared and was never to be seen again. Jennifer had been scarred for life mentally and emotionally. After Jennifer came home from the hospital, her parents tried to restore their relationship with their daughter, but things were never the same. Jennifer could never get over the hurt she went through with her parents kicking her out, her abusive relationship, and her loss of the baby.

Two years later, Jennifer was found dead with a needle in her arm. She was unable to pay her debts to her dealer, so the dealer gave her rat poison for her last hit. Although Jennifer lost her life at a young age, her death caused her parents to truly give their lives to God.

For a long time, the family blamed Maggie for Jennifer's troubles. Maggie herself cursed the gift God had given her. But once Mrs. Vaughn had given her life over to God, Maggie was able to accept her gift as something good God could use.

~

One morning, Erica received a call from her sister Maggie. "What!" Erica almost dropped the phone.

"I dreamed about fish! Someone in your family is about to have a baby, Erica!"

Erica screamed. "Maggie don't tell me that! My stuff is too old to be having a baby."

"You are not the one who is pregnant. I dreamed it is one of the boys. I did see you, but you were looking at your boys."

"Okay, I will call you back in an hour. I have to find out who it is!" Erica started yelling in the house. "Johnston, Johnston! That was Maggie!"

"Calm down, calm down," Johnston said.

"Lord, have mercy. One of those boys is going to have a baby."

"Do you even know who it is? You could be jumping to conclusions. It could be Nolan."

"Yeah, and it could be Roderick or Greg. I know that April girl is only after my baby's money."

"Erica, you are getting hysterical, and you don't even know the facts. Didn't we just have this conversation a few weeks ago? Here you are jumping to conclusions and judging April before getting to know her."

"Oh god, I'm sorry." Erica reached out to Johnston and put her head in his chest. "I just don't want him to make the same mistakes." Johnston held Erica tight. "I know, Erica, but God doesn't make mistakes. When a child comes into this world, it is meant to be here for God's glory and honor. Whoever it is, be different than the world.

We love on them no matter what. They have to learn from their own mistakes if they don't learn from ours. Remember, instruct a child in the way they should go, and that is what we've done. You have to let go, Erica. These boys are not children anymore. They are grown men and have to make choices for themselves. You can't rescue them from every situation they get into."

"I know, but I still have to find out who it is."

"And you have a right to know, but then what? Are you going to ostracize him like your mother did your sister, or are you going to use godly wisdom and let God handle this situation for us?"

Erica nervously answered, "I am going to let God handle it, but I can still call them to find out, can't I?"

"Yes, you can still call them, but do it lovingly and not condemningly. That's how many of our young people run away from the church. It is not for us to judge, it is for us to lift them, encourage them, and show them the love of Christ. They may know the way, but they still need us to encourage them to get back up again and live for God without compromising or lowering their standards. Love them back into the fold. Love them until they come back to Christ. That is one thing your mother was not able to do for your sister because she didn't have the love of Christ in her life at the time."

"Thanks for loving me back into the fold."

"You are most welcome."

Erica called her sons one by one to see if any of them knew of the pending birth.

"Mother, after our third child, Marie got her tubes tied, so it's not us."

"Oh, Lord!"

"Mom don't get all hysterical."

"Nolan, I'm not getting hysterical. I just know that if it isn't you, then one of my other sons is having a baby out of wedlock."

"I know it's hard to swallow, but your sons have to make their own mistakes. Let them be men. Just like you always told us, if you are old enough to lay, you are old enough to pay. Just call me when you find out. I have to go to practice now."

"So, how are the A's treating you?"

"Great. I love every minute of it. Guess what my batting average is this year?"

"I don't have to guess, it's 332."

"I love you, mom. Don't stress out. Everything will work out even if it doesn't look like it now."

"I love you too, baby."

Nolan was always the encourager. As much as he had to over-come, he always encouraged everyone around him. His teammates loved him. They nicknamed him Chaplain because he prayed before every game.

~

"What!"

Erica pulled the phone away from her ear. "Greg, stop screaming in my ear."

There was silence for ten seconds. "Aunt Maggie didn't see my face. I don't even have time for sex, let alone girls right now. Once I get over my probation at Baying, I may start dating then, but you know me. I'm not going out like that! Have you talked to Nolan or Roderick?"

"I have already talked to Nolan. He said it's not him. Marie had her tubes tied after Nolan, Jr."

"Aww man! Mom, you didn't have to tell me all that! Just a simple 'No, it's not Nolan' would have been cool."

Erica started to laugh. "Well, you know me. I'm detail oriented. It's all or nothing, son."

"Anyway, call me when you find out about Roderick, the big baller, shot caller, and I do mean that literally."

"I'll let you know for sure when I find out."

Erica didn't know how to take this process of elimination. 'What was Roderick thinking?' she thought. After all he's been through, he fell for this mess. She prayed and asked God for guidance. She didn't want to judge the situation too harshly, but she wanted to be that example of love to Roderick and April.

Erica called Roderick's dorm phone, and the voicemail came on. Please leave your name and number, and I will get back with you as soon as possible. God bless.

"Roderick, this is your mother. Call me as soon as possible. Your Aunt Maggie called today and gave me some news that I need to discuss with you about your relationship with April."

~

April stood next to the answering machine, disturbed by the message Roderick's mother left.

"Oh really?" she said aloud to herself. "Well, he won't be getting this message. As a matter of fact, our trip is going to shorten quite a bit—like we will not be going to see you at all, mommy dearest."

The day before Roderick and April were to arrive in Georgia, April went through with her plan to disrupt the flow. "Roderick, I don't feel so good. I've been throwing up all night, and I have the chills. I think I'm coming down with the flu, and I don't think I'm going to be able to make the trip."

Roderick rubbed her face as she lay in bed. "When did you start feeling sick?" He touched her forehead to see if she had a fever.

"I told you, last night."

Roderick poked out his lips to make fun of April. "You want me to make you feel better?" Roderick laughed as April tried to look pitiful.

"Yes. Can you take care of me?" "Yes, baby. I can take care of you."

"I'm sorry we have to postpone the trip."

Roderick jumped up from the side of the bed. "Why do we have to postpone the trip?"

April sat up from the bed, looking upset. "Because I'm sick, and I can't fly like this."

Roderick put his hands behind his head. "Babe, I know you are sick and all, and I know you were looking forward to meeting my parents, but I haven't seen my family in months. I may not get a chance to see them after the season starts. You can't expect me to change my plans just because you have the flu."

April looked at Roderick like she couldn't believe what he had just said. "No, I expect you to care about me and want to take care of me when I don't feel well. I should be considered first, Rick!" April yelled at the top of her lungs.

"April, I love you, honey, and I'm here for you. If it were something more serious, I'd stay right by your side and take care of you, but you have the flu. It's not like you are dying. I'll go get you some medicine before I leave, and I'll call you when I land. You are a big girl, and you can take care of yourself."

April was upset, but she tried to hide it. "Don't bother. I'll take care of myself. I'll feel better by tomorrow, and I will be making that trip with you."

"That's the spirit! But make sure you are well because if my mom finds out you came down knowing you were sick, oh boy. That is one woman you don't want to have around when you are sick."

"I'll be fine. It might have been something I ate. Food poisoning."

"Let me know if you need anything. I am going to finish packing. We have to get up bright and early."

As Roderick walked out of April's dorm room, she pulled up her pillow to her face. "Yippee."

Roderick returned to his dorm and heard his phone ringing. "Hello?"

"Boy, have you lost your mind? Why haven't you returned any of my phone calls?"

"Mom, I haven't received any messages from you."

"Roderick, I have left three messages in the past two weeks. I even called Jarred to see if anything happened to you. He said he's been seeing you in the hallways."

"Mom, I haven't seen Jarred. He's been gone for a week."

"I don't know what's going on out there, but you better find out. You need to fix your answering service."

"Mom, I promise you, nothing is wrong with my answering service, and I haven't gotten any messages from you, but I will check it out."

"All right. I've been trying to reach you about some news your Aunt Maggie told me. I think I will just wait until you get here to discuss it. I can't wait for you to get here."

"I can't wait either, mom. I've been gone too long without visiting home. I can't wait for you to meet April. I think she's the one."

"Well, we will discuss all of that when you get here." Erica disturbed.

"Okay. Tell dad I said hi. See you guys tomorrow. God willing."

It didn't take much for Erica to become sarcastic. "Oh yes, God is willing, baby. He is so willing for truth, and the truth shall set you free."

Roderick was now confused by his mother's remarks. "Okay, Mom. We'll see you tomorrow."

"Bye baby."

After getting off the phone with his mom, Roderick called his friend Jarred. "Jarred, my mom said she called you."

"Your mom did call, and I left a message on your answering machine telling you to call her."

"Man, this is strange. Do me a favor. Call me and leave a message to see if my machine is working."

"Okay, hold on. I have three-way, so I'll call and merge the call."

As the phone rang, Roderick's messaging service came on instantly. Jared was able to leave a message just fine.

"Thanks, Jarred. Something is going on. I'll call you when I get back from Georgia."

"All right dude. Stay positive."

"Will do, will do."

~

The flight to Georgia was uneventful, but as soon as Roderick stepped off the plane, cheers of celebration rang loud. Banners, signs, friends, and family were there to greet him.

"Hi mom! How are you?" Roderick hugged his mom, and April tried to be on her best behavior. Nolan and Greg then greeted Roderick, along with Johnston and Nolan's three children.

"Hi, Uncle Roderick," Nolan's three children said so sweetly.

"Oh! My, you guys are so cute. You look just like your mommy."

"Shut up, man," Nolan said with a grin.

Roderick stepped back from everyone and pulled April next to him. "Everyone, this is April." One by one, April shook their hands and stepped back to her comfort zone, which was right next to Roderick.

"Well, let's get going. We have to get your luggage," Erica said. "How many pieces did you bring? Well, it really doesn't matter. We brought the van."

"Mom, you didn't bring one of the church vans, did you?"

"Why not? We had all these people who wanted to come and see you. It didn't make sense to drive three cars. Besides, it is a fifteen-passenger van. Even your big head can fit in it."

"Dad, you need to do something with this woman. She hasn't changed a bit."

Johnston smiled from ear to ear. "Man don't get me in the middle of that one."

Getting home was no quiet task. As soon as everyone got into the van, Erica started drilling April, but like a lawyer, April's answers sounded scripted. Erica's first impression of April was not a good one.

"So, tell me April, where do your parents live?"

"They live in Puerto Rico. They are natives and don't want to leave their home. I tried to get them to move to California, but they wouldn't come. Besides, we really don't see eye to eye in our belief systems. They are Catholic, and I am Christian. It was hard for them to understand my conversion."

"I am sorry to hear that. Do you have any siblings?"

"Yes, I have two sisters and one brother, just like you, Mrs. Manning."

"That's Mrs. Matthews, dear." Erica turned back toward the front of the van and didn't speak another word until they arrived home. Johnston and Roderick both knew that Erica's silence was not a good sign. When they arrived at the front door, April stepped out of the van.

"Wow, baby. I didn't expect your parents' home to be so big. It's gorgeous!"

"Well, later you can tell my mom that to make up for calling her Mrs. Manning instead of Mrs. Matthews."

"I didn't know that I was saying her name wrong."

"Come on, April. I've told you about my family a million times. You study law, you should be taking in the details and thinking before you speak."

By this time, steam was coming out of April's ears. "You know what? I know your family is important to you, but the Bible says that a man should leave his parents and cling to his wife. You act like you have never left home."

Roderick turned to April and looked her in the eye. "Well, if you ever become my wife, then we'll talk about it."

"How can you even say such a thing? We've talked about getting married, and we've even...you know."

"April, as much as I am into you, that one time will be the only time until we get married. I have repented and asked God to forgive me, so I'm good. I hope you have truly repented too because I don't plan on making that mistake with you or anyone else again."

"I can't believe you are saying this!"

"I'm not saying that I don't want to be with you, but we both know what we did was wrong. This weekend isn't about us, it's about spending time with family. By the way, you and I will be telling my parents what we did, and we'll let them know that we have repented."

"Why do they need to know? We have repented to God. Isn't

that enough?"

"Sure, that's enough, but my family didn't raise me to cower in my sin. We talk to each other and discuss our downfalls. We encourage each other to continue walking before the Lord even when we fall. Yes, we all have sins that we tell God alone, but when the time is right, God may use our experiences we hide to help someone else. Us sleeping together is not something I want to keep from them because my mother will ask me if I am still a virgin, and I will not lie to her."

April contorted her face to a confused look. "I just don't understand you," she said as she walked away. "Whatever."

Roderick gazed at the dust behind April as she walked away and then focused in on the house next door—a sore reminder of what he had endured. At that very moment, true repentance took place in his heart. He had forgotten how God had spared his life in that basement of torture. Roderick fell to his knees and cried out to God. Erica looked out the window and saw her son. She could see the transformation take place. He finally looked peaceful and untroubled. "What's going on?" Johnston saw Erica looking out the window.

"I think your son is releasing himself from some burdens," Erica stated happily.

"Do you want me to go talk to him?"

"No. I believe he is going to come to us. When, I don't know, but when it's time, he will come."

They looked over to the house that once belonged to Mr. Hughes, and it looked so different now. There were children playing in the yard. A father and mother watched their children play. There was laughter instead of sorrow, and a family instead of a lonesome, sick, and murderous man. There was love instead of destruction and death.

Roderick started to carry in April's luggage. "You want me to help you, son?"

"No thanks, Dad. I got them, but I would like to talk to you and Mom tonight."

It startled Johnston that Erica was right. "Your mother said you would want to talk to us eventually. She said wait until you came to us first."

"Well, that's Mom. Just let her know for me." "Okay."

"By the way, where is April sleeping?"

"She's sleeping in the playroom on the couch—with the kids. Nolan and Marie will take the guest bedroom. You and Greg will either sleep down here or you guys can sleep in my office. There is a pullout bed in there."

"Things haven't changed much. Don't tell me Mom put you out on the couch already."

"No, man. When I'm studying and fasting, I sleep in there."

"Thanks, I want to be just like you when I grow up."

"Be like Jesus. He's the example to follow."

"I know, I'm just messing around."

~

The night was young, and April knew what was coming. She tried to sneak up the stairs, but Roderick grabbed her hand and guided her into the living room. Erica and Johnston were already seated, and Roderick and April sat themselves across from them in the smaller loveseat. Heads twisted and turned, and silence remained for at least a minute or more. Erica was visibly tired of the squirming.

"What are your plans for the future?"

"Mrs. Matthews, I'm not sure of what you mean."

"Ms. Thing, I have been around the way and have done and seen a lot of things. My son would not have given you the time of day if you weren't coming correct and right. You know his potential and you know that if the Lord says the same, he will be going to the NBA. So, let me rephrase the question in a way that you will understand:

"What are your plans for my son?"

"Wait a minute, Mom. You have April all wrong. We love each other, and I know she is not with me because I play ball. She has a good heart and loves the Lord."

Erica stood up. "Boy, open your eyes. If you know nothing else, you should know I judge character very well."

Johnston quickly jumped in the conversation. "Hold on now," he said. "Erica, may I speak to you in the kitchen?" Johnston and Erica walked into the kitchen. "Erica, why are you doing this? You're being harsh."

"Johnston, that girl is wrong for him. She is pregnant with his child, and she is going to make him pay for it for the rest of his life. How is she going to act when she knows that she is pregnant? When she finds out, she is going to change."

Johnston couldn't believe what Erica was saying. He had never felt this disappointment in her before. "Erica, what if your sister is wrong?"

"Johnston, in all the years that Maggie has known about her gift, she has never been wrong. All of the children that were conceived and delivered from this womb, my sister Maggie let me know I was going to have them. My sister is not wrong, and I just know it."

"Okay, Erica. If what you say is true, then don't go after April as an investigator. You are going to alienate Roderick if you haven't already. He loves April, and he brought her here to meet his mother. Show him different. Show him some respect because he is a grown man who planned for his own life. I know you want to protect him because of what happened in the past, but you are going about this the wrong way. And if you don't stop right now, you are going to lose him."

Erica heard Johnston, but she was determined to show Roderick that April was not right for him. "I am going to expose that devil for what she is. It's going to hurt because he will have to deal with her for the rest of that child's life."

"Erica, he is a grown man. He slept with her, and now he has to be responsible in taking care of that child, if she's pregnant."

"Johnston, I just want you to know he is going to need you as a father, a man, and an example of what it means to be a parent. I beg you to listen to me this once."

"You know and he knows I will be there for him. The question is, does he know at this point that you will be there for him and will not judge him?"

Erica stopped and looked at Johnston. He was concerned. Together, they walked back into the living room as if their lives were hanging in the balance.

"Roderick, your mom has something she needs to tell you, and I think you need to listen to what she has to say."

"Dad, I know that you and mom mean well. But I can feel the tension between mom and April. She just met her, and she's already trying to interrogate her. How do you think that makes us feel? Did you even consider that I know what I'm doing, and I know how to take care of myself? I love April, and if God wants us together, then we will be together. But I won't marry someone God hasn't sent."

"Well, Roderick, tell me what you are going to do with the child she's carrying?"

"What? What are you talking about?"

Finally, April stood to defend herself from the darts that were being thrown her way. "What in the world are you talking about? I am not pregnant! I can't believe you, a saved woman, would accuse me of anything like this. If I didn't know better, I'd think you were jealous of the relation- ship I have with your son."

Roderick grabbed April's arm and pulled her back onto the couch. "April, you just took it too far," he said disappointedly.

"How can you say that I have taken this too far when she accused me with no proof?"

Roderick was up on his feet now. "April, calm down. Let's talk about this."

Erica was now sitting at the edge of the couch, ready for battle. "Roderick, your Aunt Maggie called me three weeks ago. She let me know that one of my sons was having a baby. It's not Nolan, and it's not Greg. Marie can't have any more children, and Greg doesn't have a girlfriend, so that leaves you. Are you still a virgin?"

Roderick looked at April with an "I told you so" expression. "Well, that's why I wanted to talk to you and Dad," Roderick

admitted. "We did have sex, and we did ask God to forgive us. We haven't done anything since that one time. It took place a little over a month ago, but I am pretty sure that April is not pregnant because she's taking birth control pills."

Now Johnston was curious. "April, how long have you been taking birth control pills?" Johnston asked.

April answered hesitantly, "For a few months or so." She didn't know what the right answer would be.

"Roderick, did you know about this?"

"No, I didn't. I thought she just needed to take them that night. I don't know anything about birth control pills."

"Did you use a condom?"

The questions were making Roderick frustrated and tense. "No! It just happened!" he said angrily.

"Boy, don't you raise your voice up in here! First of all, women don't start taking birth control pills unless they are planning to have sex. And someone who takes birth control pills months before they have sex is suspect to me!"

Everyone was silent. Roderick could see that Johnston was holding back Erica from slapping him silly.

"Listen, Roderick. You will have to decide about whether you want to continue a relationship with April. It's obvious that she has been lying to you. Regular birth control pills don't work overnight. You have to have them in your system for at least a month in order to avoid getting pregnant. Now either she's lying about taking the birth control pills, or she's been lying to you about her intentions of getting with you and planning to have sex with you. Someone has been lying to you, and you've just been so blind. You are going to have to figure this out yourself. I appreciate you being honest with us and letting us know. God loves you, and we love you no matter what. We under- stand what you are going through and we will go through it with you. We are here to help you in any way we can."

Johnston took his turn to talk. "Roderick, there are consequences to sin," Johnston turned to April. "And if you are pregnant, April, then you guys have a lot to work out. You know, most of the time I try to stay clear, but even I am wondering what your intentions are with Roderick."

"Well, Mr. and Mrs. Matthews, you have made it very clear how you feel about me, but I have to ask: is judging me godly? Yes, we did make a mistake, but we repented. There is no way I'm pregnant. Yes, Roderick and I have a lot to discuss because I don't know if I want to be part of this family anymore. You have done nothing but downgrade me since we arrived here. You have not embraced me like parents should. Roderick and I love each other, and only God can change that. You should be ashamed of yourselves. Take the speck out of your own eyes."

The room fell silent. April contemplated the actions and the following through that needed to take place. There was no turning back now. The game had to play itself out. Inside, anxiety rose in her, and she cringed like a child making her first speech in front of an entire school. Tears of confusion rolled down her face, and her petite frame stormed out of the room to make it appear as if she had won this round.

"¿Por qué usted incluso juzgará me? Why would you even judge me? Puede incluso no ha obtenido conocerme. You haven't even had the chance to get to know me. Usted solo cumplieron me hoy. You just met me today."

The swift thought of grabbing April and ringing her neck flashed right before Erica's eyes. She immediately repented aloud when the thought came across her mind.

"No, Johnston! I know she didn't just walk out of here speaking Spanish. No, she didn't just walk away from this conversation." Erica was frustrated and angry.

"Honey just let it go for now. We can talk about this tomorrow."

There was a time when Roderick would have sat down and let this happen. But Roderick was a man now, and he rose up to defend his girlfriend. "No, we won't be discussing this anymore because tomorrow we will be leaving, and that's final. I now know that it was a mistake to bring April here. Maybe it was too soon. Maybe April is right about you judging us. All I know is that I came home to show April what a family is all about, and tonight you blew it. Especially you, Mom. You never even gave her a chance. Whatever happens between us, we will take care of it ourselves."

As Roderick turned to walk up the stairs, Erica called to him. He stopped and turned toward his mother. She was almost in tears.

"Son, you are blind. Open your eyes, Roderick. You make mistakes in life but make them and learn from them. Trust me, you don't want to find out the hard way. You can leave tomorrow but know what I am saying is true. April is not being honest with you. We love you, and we always look out for you. Please pray and listen to God about your relationship, son. I'm begging you."

Once again, there was only silence. Erica's thoughts kept her awake all night. She reflected on what happened that evening and prayed.

~

The next morning while everyone was asleep, Roderick and April left to catch a flight back to California. They ate a light breakfast of toast and eggs at the airport café and boarded the plane. The rumbling of the plane's engines reminded April of her rumbling stomach. The plane's wheels began to move, and the force of the takeoff was undoubtedly more intense than usual. As the nose of the 747 began to rise, the sudden surge of salty saliva rushed through her mouth glands. She grabbed the vomit bag and proceeded to bring up all that she had eaten for breakfast and what she had for dinner the previous night. After vomiting, she raised her torso and looked as though she had gone through World War III. With sweat dripping from her brow, she mumbled a few words. Roderick's concern was expressed most emphatically.

"What's going on with you?"

"That food I ate must have been bad," April said, breathing heavily. "As soon as the plane took off, I got sick."

"Well, lay back and I'll ask the flight attendant to get you some ginger ale." From there, the flight was less eventful.

They arrived in Los Angeles safely. Roderick dropped off April at her dorm and gave her a kiss on the forehead. He walked to his own dorm room, which was half a block away.

April dropped her bags in the doorway of her room. Exhausted, she headed straight to her twin-sized bed and flopped down as though she had completed a twenty-six-mile marathon. The phone rang, but she didn't pick it up. With her face in the pillow, she waved off the phone and didn't care that she could barely hear the message that was being recorded. She fell asleep. Later that afternoon, a knock on her door startled her.

"Hold on. Just hold on!" April screamed aloud. She opened the door to find a tall, handsome man standing as confidently as a man could. He was smooth, chocolate, and looked like he was in his mid-thirties. April, who was five-foot-six, looked up at the man. "Can I help you?" she asked sarcastically.

His voice soft but masculine. A woman on the prowl probably would have invited him in, but April recognized him. "I have a message for you." He handed her the sealed paper and stood there waiting. April turned and slammed the door in his face. It was a matter of time before she knew he would contact her. 'Meet me at the Boulevard Café, 6 o'clock sharp.'

It was already five o'clock, and from Westwood to Crenshaw and King, it would take some time to get there, especially on a Sunday.

What does he want now? she thought.

As much as she despised him, she was afraid to disappoint him. She could not break free from his evil and tantalizing grip. He could ruin her life and the plans she had for Roderick. Roderick was her future cash-cow, and the plan was to take him for everything she could possibly get out of him. She had to meet this man. It was too dangerous not to.

~

An hour later, April arrived and greeted the man. "All right, I'm here." April pushed out air in a huff.

"Sit down, baby. Your man wants to see how you're doing. I miss you so much, but we have bigger plans, don't we? I just want to know how everything is going. I haven't heard from you in two weeks, and you haven't returned any of my phone calls. I just need to know what's going on."

Reluctant to give any details, she thought of what she needed to tell him to keep him from being suspicious of her own motives. "We just came back from Georgia. I met his mother and her husband and his brothers. That meeting didn't go so well, but it appears he is in love with me because he chose my side. We left after being there only one day. We were supposed to stay for two weeks."

His laugh was cunning and sure. "My, my, the boy is in love. I knew my baby could reel him in. As soon as he is drafted, the money will start rolling in. Keep up the good work. Our plans will succeed."

Determination was the only way for her to get rid of them both, she thought. She needed the money, and Roderick was her only option. "I need to get back. I'm pretty sure he will be looking for me soon." April stood up to leave.

"Okay, baby." He pulled her close and stuck his tongue down her throat. In his mind, April was his, but she had other plans. Still, she made sure her demeanor never flinched or made him believe otherwise. For the rest of the evening, April was undisturbed.

~

Roderick didn't call or show up to her dorm room. He had not moved from his bed. Thoughts of his mother, family, April, and what had transpired between them plagued him like a disease. He was torn and confused. April had not given him any reason to be suspicious, and his mother had never lied to him before. He didn't know what to believe.

Had his relationship with April moved too fast? Did he really seek God about dating her? Was he blinded by lust? He could do nothing but lay there. He was paralyzed by his emotions and his inability to reason through the situation. School would not start for another two weeks. From Sunday to Wednesday, he barely slept or ate. He ignored April. She constantly called and came to his dorm room, but he refused to see or talk to her.

During this time, Roderick slept a lot and had a dream. Roderick's dream:

I was at a basketball game with three seconds on the clock. The ball was passed to me to make the last basket of the NCAA championship. I bounced the ball once and set up to shoot as time stood still. Everything froze around me. My body was able to move, but I was unable to push the basketball to make the shot. It felt right, and I knew that it would go in for the win. For one minute straight, I was a mime without the white face makeup. Turning my body from left to right, I thought that maybe I was dead.

"No, Roderick," a voice said. "This is your life. You are at a standstill, and you aren't able to go any- where or do anything without me."

Instant fear rocked my body, and I fell on my face like so many others had done in the Old Testament times.

"God is that you?" Cowering, I was prone on the gym floor.

"Would it help if I said no?" the voice said. "No, because I know it is you, Lord." "Fortunately, Roderick, I'm who you need me

to be, and I like the fact you have bowed before me." The scripture instantly came to my mind:

"My sheep know my voice and a stranger they will not follow." "Oh my god. I'm lost forever," I cried out. "I've turned to the dark side." I was sobbing uncontrollably.

"Yes, I am your God now. Listen to me, your mother is wrong about April. You know her better than anyone. She will be by your side forever, no matter what happens. She'll never leave you nor for- sake you like your mother did. I have a loophole for all your troubles to go away. You know, God doesn't want you to know His secrets. He only gives His secrets to those who have not sinned or fallen a little short of His expectations. That word you read is written by men and is not inspired by God."

"No, that is not true. God's word is true, and those men were inspired by the Holy Spirit."

"That is what man wants you to think. Do you really think God would create an awful world like this? God is perfect and true. He put me here to rule over you and to choose the one who will rise up and whom I want to degrade to nothing. I chose you to achieve, Roderick. I chose you for the loophole because I knew that your eyes would be open to the truth of God's plan. You succeed because I allow you to."

"Satan, you are a liar, and the truth is not in you. Get thee behind me, Satan. You have no place in my mind, thoughts, life, or who I will become. You are already defeated by the blood of Jesus Christ. You are the father of lies, and I bind you in the name of Jesus Christ of Nazareth. God's Word says that whatever I bind on earth, it will be bound in heaven. The blood of Jesus is against you."

In that instance, Roderick woke up to a ringing phone. "Hello?" "Roderick, I have been calling you for the past three days," April said frustratingly. "Where have you been?"

Roderick was still shaken by the dream, but he spoke clearly. "April, I have been soul searching. Are you alone?"

"For a few hours. Why do you want to know?"

As Roderick talked to her on the phone, he was getting dressed to leave. "Give me about thirty minutes. I'm coming over. I need to talk to you."

Roderick hung up the phone without saying goodbye. April froze and just listened to the dial tone blaze through the receiver. She didn't know what to make of the call.

Roderick stopped by a drugstore and then headed back to April's dorm room. "Hi baby." Unrelenting in his quest to know the truth, he walked in and handed her a box. "I need you to take this pregnancy test."

April was stunned. As she made her way to the bathroom, Roderick followed.

"Just pee in the cup and dip the stick." As she followed the directions, she couldn't help but wonder if he knew more about what she was up to. Even to her surprise, two blue lines appeared.

Roderick walked out of the bathroom and out of April's dorm room without saying a word.

Chapter 14

Grace & Justice Revealed

THE NEXT MORNING, Roderick was back on a plane to Georgia— without April. She didn't even know he was gone. She went to his dorm room, and when Jarred saw her in the hallway, he told her that Roderick had gone back to Georgia. April couldn't get a hold of Roderick, so she was bold and called Erica. But still no one answered her phone calls. The only person she could turn to, was the man who had schemed with her from the start.

"I have to talk to you now. I need you to come and get me right."

It wasn't until they were face to face that she finally realized he did not care or love her at all.

"I'm pregnant, and Roderick has left for Georgia. I don't know if he is ever going to come back."

'Woman, have you lost your mind? You weren't supposed to sleep with him. You were only supposed to make him fall in love with you. I should throw you in a shark pit. How stupid can you be? You have ruined everything." He slapped her. "You are supposed to be my woman. Now, how are you supposed to leave him with a kid hanging over your head? I'm taking you to get an abortion tomorrow."

"No! I will not kill this baby. You can kill me all you want, but I will not get rid of this baby. Are you that cold of a man that you would get rid of your own grandchild? This is your flesh and blood I am carrying. How could you even think of doing such a thing? I know I've done a lot of stupid and wrong in my life, but I'm not a murderer."

"Do you have any idea what this is going to do?" And then, it was just like a lightbulb flickering on and off. His mind clicked on to how he could use this to their advantage. "Maybe we can use this as leverage after all. He's going to have to pay you until that child is eighteen. This is better than even I imagined."

April was sickened by the sight of Gary. She walked out of his apartment while he had gone to the bathroom.

Walking down the street going nowhere, she continued to cry uncontrollably. Any shot at happiness was gone. All she could think about was how she had screwed up her life. It was awful to realize that she knew the Word of God but had not even once thought about applying any of it to her own life.

~

Roderick arrived in Atlanta confused. All he could think about was the dream he had where he talked to the devil.

He sat at the doorsteps of his parents' home. He had not told them he was coming. He walked in with Erica unaware of his presence. The house was silent, and Johnston was nowhere to be found. He stood in the doorway of the living room.

"Oh my god, Roderick, you scared me. What are you doing here?" As Erica continued to sit on the couch, Roderick kneeled down and laid his head on her lap.

"I'm so stupid, mom. I can't believe I was that stupid." Erica raised his head up. "What's going on, Roderick?"

"She's pregnant." The sigh could be heard all around the house. In that moment, Erica was no longer the mom. She became the no-nonsense investigator. She immediately honed in on what needed to be done.

"Get up, Roderick. Let me make this very clear. You will take care of that child. You will share the responsibility and have a say in raising that child. First, we will get a lawyer to represent you in court so that you can get joint custody. I know just the right person. You will give me all the information you can on this girl. For some reason, God is telling me that April is not in this alone. I can't put my finger on it.

You were the target and she was the bait and you fell hook, line, and sinker."

"Mom don't rub it in."

"Roderick, get over yourself. You have to learn that everyone is not on your side. The enemy is here to steal, kill, and destroy as many lives as he can. It's time for you to take your life back. Yes, you will have my help and support, but you will now have to truly stand as a man and take back what the devil has stolen from you in the name of Jesus. Do you know how you beat the devil? You get in that Word, you get down on your knees and pray, and you turn away that plate. Then and only then will you hear from heaven and receive guidance and direction. *"Seek ye first the kingdom—"*

"The kingdom of God and His righteousness." Roderick completed.

"Roderick, you know the Word. Start applying it to your life and stop giving lip service. Learning and seeking God's face doesn't stop after you repent and accept Christ into your heart. It's just the beginning. Every time you fail your test, it's because you lose focus on God and His awesome power. Instead of looking at your circumstances, watch God move on your behalf. You're looking at how you are going to solve this on your own, instead of trusting and believing that God can do the impossible."

"Mom," Roderick said. "I didn't know she lied to me. I didn't know that sleeping with her one time would land me a baby."

"As long as you are alive, you have an opportunity to get up and succeed the next time. What you learn is the reward. The problem is that most young adults think we older folk have no clue about what you go through. We have gone through this and more. Whether it's a parent who is a believer or not, we've all gone through or have known others who have gone through these things. If you would just take the time to listen to us and understand that God is just waiting for you to seek Him, you'd be all right. All parents want their children to do is make good choices. Making a good choice is seeking out good counsel—unconditional counsel—from heaven before we make a move. We can avoid so much drama and heartache. It may take you awhile, but you will get it. I just pray you get it before it's too late."

Roderick slammed himself on the couch as Johnston walked in the door.

"Whoa, what happened?" Johnston said.

Erica got up from the couch, kissed Johnston, and headed toward the stairs. "I will leave you two alone. Roderick can explain to you what's going on. I'll be down in an hour or so to prepare dinner. I have to go pray."

Erica reached the top of the stairs. She could hear Roderick sobbing again, while Johnston stayed quiet until he finished. Johnston continued to be quiet. He didn't want to discourage Roderick in his hour of need. He stood up and walked over to the fireplace.

"Don't go down the road of being seduced by the enemy. You have a child on the way. You have to finish school. You have a lot of decisions to make. Only you and God can figure out the answers. Your mother and I can only help you by praying for you. Do you understand what I am telling you?"

Roderick stayed on the floor with his head hanging down and his lips hanging even lower. He raised his head briefly. "I'm going to have to seek God for those answers."

"You hit the nail on the head, man. You are going to have to turn away the plate, turn off the television, turn off the practices, and turn off everything that is a distraction and a hindrance. I guarantee you that God will tell you exactly what you need to do and how to handle this situation. He'll teach you how to be a good father, man of God, and future husband."

"Oh, no! I will not be marrying April. That's for sure. She has lied to me one too many times, and I can't trust her anymore."

"Well, son, just remember that April will be the mother of your child whether you like it or not. Now you have to learn to respect her. You may not like how she lied to you, but if you lay, you pay, and I suggest you be the man your father never was and be responsible for raising your child the way that he or she should go. It's up to you to be a better man than me and your father. Learn from our mistakes. Learn from how you saw your father treat your brothers and your mother.

You have the potential to be a great basketball player, and with that comes great responsibility because trust me, unless you stay rooted and grounded in God, money will change you. Look at what it has done to your father and how it has destroyed the relationship you had. It's great to have money, but don't let it rule you or your decision to be the man that God wants you to be. Remember, we have to be very careful about what we ask for. We just might get it because God is faithful and answers prayer."

"Well, I only have a couple of weeks before I go back. I need to have some answers and a plan."

"Like I said, take this opportunity to seek those answers from God."

Johnston pulled Roderick up from the floor and hugged him. As always, it was a genuine gesture. They were no longer just friends; they had become father and son.

~

There were two thunderstorms back-to-back. It hadn't rained like this in ten years. Lightning struck a generator so loud that it could be heard from miles away. Raindrops that were the size of marbles fell from the sky, and thunder moved the ground like an earthquake. The wind blew at a rate of forty miles per hour and whisked through the trees, swaying them north and east. Within an hour, the storm had dissipated and moved into the neighboring city, where they too would feel the wrath of God's firmament.

It wasn't until the next morning that any damage could be assessed. There was mostly roof damage to the older houses, but amid the storm, a single window was broken at the Matthews' residence due to a tree branch that had broken off.

"Thank God for His mercy and grace. That's the only damage we sustained."

Erica looked at the window Johnston was taping up. "We are blessed. Where is Roderick?"

"When I got up this morning, he was walking out the door to go jogging. When he came back, he came into the study to pray. I prayed with him for an hour, but he is still up there. I think this situation really has him troubled. While he was held hostage, he might have prayed, but then his body shut down. But now that he's free, he's conscious and alert enough to seek God about what to do. If he doesn't come down, just know that he's decided to fast. He told me last night that he needed to go back to California with a plan and guidance from God. So that is what he is seeking for right now."

Erica routinely kissed her husband every morning and night, but now she felt the urge to kiss him once more to show gratitude. "Thank you," she said.

Johnston didn't have to say anything in return. She knew that he loved her just by the way he looked at her and the way he wrapped his loving arms around her.

~

Roderick felt trapped and helpless. He cried unto the Lord. Balled up into a fetal position, he could do nothing but pray.

As much as she wanted to, Erica could not save her son from this, just like when he had been taken. This time, he was going to have to seek God on his own.

Several times during the week, Erica and Johnston could hear Roderick and the Holy Spirit moving on him. Erica would rejoice in the living room, as Roderick would speak in tongues unto the Lord.

Sunday morning came. Roderick stepped out of the room bright and early. Erica came out of the bedroom at the same time. They both looked at each other and walked down the stairs in silence. It was apparent to them both that sometimes you don't have to speak to know what the other person is thinking. It was a look of forgiveness and love that only a mother could provide a child.

~

The rest of the morning and evening on the plane ride back to California, God continued to prepare him for what was ahead.

It wasn't until after basketball practice that Roderick knocked on April's dorm room. She was surprised to see him. He had compassion, but the intimate love he once had for her was gone. When his parents had divorced, it seemed impossible to understand the complexities of an unevenly yoked relationship. The look he gave his mother yesterday morning acknowledged that truth and more. He understood what his mother had to go through with his biological father.

April welcomed Roderick into her living space. As they sat, she tried to apologize, but just as abruptly, Roderick interrupted her apology.

"I know enough about you to know that you will keep the baby. Now, it's a matter of whether this is going to be done like adults, or will we have to go to court?"

Roderick sat back in the chair and waited for a response.

April twirled her thumbs. "Roderick, I do plan on keeping the baby, but I don't know what my plans are. I don't know if I can finish school right now. It may be too much for me to handle school and this pregnancy. I may have to put that on hold."

Even though she sounded convincing, he couldn't trust her.

"I understand it may be difficult, and I will be there for you every step of the way, but I want to make it clear that I am not going to quit school. God willing, when I get drafted, then and only then will I consider providing financial assistance before the baby is born. As you know, there are no guarantees. I think the stupid mistake you made was lying to me in the first place, and that is what killed our relationship. Just because we are having a child does not mean that I will fall for your lies again. I will never trust you with my heart again. I will respect you as the mother of our child, but that's it."

She thought her ears were deceiving her. Did he know about her plans? Did he know about his father? She stood up and walked to the door. "Get out. You are no longer welcome here. I will be moving. I will leave you messages on your voicemail to let you know my progress."

Roderick got up and walked out the door. As soon as he went to his dorm room, he called home. He thought that maybe he was too harsh. "Mom, I'm going to need you to call in that favor."

He explained the conversation he and April had. "No problem. I will call you in the morning."

It was the next afternoon that Roderick was contacted. The knock on the door was evidence he had to follow through with dealing with this situation. He couldn't believe his mother had serious connections. Roderick was determined to beat the devil, and if he had to fight, he would need as much ammunition—or evidence—as he could get.

"Mr. Rokowsky, it's nice to meet you."

At six-foot-six, he was unlike any Hungarian that Roderick had ever seen. He was white, bald, and curiously handsome. How did Mom get this man? Roderick thought.

"Likewise. First thing's first, you can call me Laszlo."

The conversation moved quickly and precisely. There was no stone unturned. Mr. Rokowsky was a private investigator that had come to know Jesus Christ through Erica witnessing to him in Georgia. Laszlo had moved to California after the Lord had taken his wife. He had moved there five years ago to be with their only son.

"Roderick, the only thing I ask of you is that you remember your salvation. Make sure you contact me if there are any changes.

Let me know when she moves. I will bring the equipment so you can record your conversations with her."

It was evident Roderick's demeanor had relaxed. "Thank you, Laszlo. I am glad you are a man of God. I want everything done well. It's not like I am trying to hurt her in any way. I just have a gut feeling something is going on, and I don't want to be lied to again."

"I understand, young man, but it will be up to you how you use the information I bring. I will call your mother and let her know your progress."

"Can I ask you a favor?" "Sure."

"Can you bring all the information to me first before you share it with my mother?"

"All right, I can do that, but I expect you to be honest and truthful about the information I gather. Remember, your mother is only doing this to protect you."

They both stood and shook hands, and Mr. Rokowsky moved swiftly out of the door.

"Wow, now that is a big white dude," Roderick said to himself out loud.

The next few weeks brought many surprises. Rumors swirled around campus that April had moved in with some guy. Roderick knew where she lived, but he had no clue who the guy was, and now he suspected that he may not be the father after all. It took a whole week for Mr. Rokowsky to finally get a good look at the man April lived with and to take pictures of him.

Roderick's suspicions about the baby's father grew, and he sought the Lord for guidance and direction more and more. Basketball season started, and Roderick's mind went into basketball mode and on making it to the pros.

After taking the pictures and recognizing the man, Mr. Rokowsky could not show the pictures to Roderick. He got on the plane to Georgia and made a visit to Erica first.

"Roderick's been calling me about the pictures. I've only been sending him pictures of April, but I had to bring the pictures of her man, to you first." He handed the package to Erica and sat back in the lounge chair.

Slowly, she opened them and was in utter shock with tears rolling down her face. She didn't know how this would affect Roderick. "Right now, we have to keep these from Roderick until basketball season is over," Erica decided. "By then, April will be close to delivering. You know, this baby may not even be his. I cannot believe that Gary would stoop this low to do something like this. He had this planned from the beginning. That devil."

Her attention diverted back to Laszlo. "Where are you staying?" "I am at the Biltmore."

"Come by the house around seven. Johnston will be home. I know he'll want to see you, and we can come up with some type of strategy. We may have to tell Roderick, but, if possible, let's hold off telling him until the season is over. We need to pray and ask God what we need to do. I'm doing all this talking without even thinking. Why didn't you interrupt me, Laszlo?"

They both laughed.

"Trust me, I am not so holy that I can't be told to seek God first. I'll take the chastening any day to stay right before the Lord."

She knew Laszlo well. As he left, she called Johnston. Unable to reach him, she left a message on his cellphone. "Hello. Laszlo is in town, and he's coming to dinner. Also, we have a situation that we need to talk about. Wait until you find out what is going on. This message would be too long if I tried to tell you now."

Later that evening, Erica, Johnston, and Laszlo sat around the kitchen table eating dinner, and Erica showed Johnston the pictures.

"Lord, have mercy. What is the man thinking? April is young enough to be his daughter."

"I know, Johnston, but what are we going to do now? I don't want Roderick to see these pictures right now. He might go off the deep end."

"I don't know if he can handle this right now either. We just have to pray."

The proof of deceit was at hand; they would wait for the right time to tell Roderick. With the season over and the victory of the NCAA Championship title and MVP behind him, this victory would be somewhat bittersweet for Roderick. He would be going to the NBA but to which team remained to be discovered.

The day had finally come when Roderick found out about Gary and April. He felt like he was in a cloud of haze; angry and disgusted—so scorned.

"The baby will be born in a week or so. Make her believe you don't know about her and your father until after the baby is born. Once it's born, we will ask for a paternity test. We will ask the judge to make your father test as well. It's not going to be an easy task to play along right now. It's going to be hard-pressed to ask the judge to give you sole custody. Right now, they could very well say that as a grandfather, he should be allowed to help the mother of his grand- child. It is going to take time and patience, and as long as God gets the glory, then everything will be just fine."

Roderick's frustration continued to show. "Mom, how do you expect me to be anything but distant from that woman? That child could very well be my father's."

"Yes, Roderick, but that child could very well be yours, and you don't want her to run off without knowing the truth. Right now, put your feelings aside and think about the child that is coming into this world. It isn't a mistake or accident; children are blessings from God. Listen for once. If this child is not yours, you'll never have to worry about it again. If this child is yours, then God wants you to honor Him and do the right thing. Believe me son, you are not going to move forward in God, your career, or your life if you have this constantly hanging over your head. Guilt and shame are not something you want to have hanging around."

"Mom, I know I have made mistakes, and trust me, I get it now. I get it now more than ever before, but this is my father. How messed up and sick is this?"

"I want you to hear me and understand. Look at Simon Peter and Judas Iscariot. Peter denied Jesus when he thought he would be punished for being associated with the Lord. He denied Jesus to the point of cursing him. Judas betrayed Jesus with a kiss. Both had to deal with guilt and shame for their denial of Christ. The difference between the two is that Peter remembered all Jesus had said and done and had true repentance in his heart. Peter lived to be a great man of God. Judas took his own life and allowed the guilt and shame to consume him. Your life is in God's hands because you have accepted and believed everything in His Word. What the devil meant for our bad, God has and will turn around for our good. No matter the outcome of the test, get back up and become that great man of God."

The next morning, Roderick called April to apologize and ask for forgiveness. It was an honest apology—an apology for God and not to April.

"Can I see you tomorrow to talk?"

Skeptical, April didn't want to pass up the chance to possibly squeeze her way back in somehow. Money was her god now. "Sure, where would you like to meet?"

"We can meet at the student library."

April didn't really want anyone to see her. "Can we meet at your dorm?"

"No, I'm not on campus anymore. My mom helped me get a place not too far from my old church." Roderick avoided telling her where he lived.

"Okay, what time?"

"We can meet about one o'clock. Afterwards, I want to take you to lunch if that's all right."

"That would be great. See you tomorrow."

April was all smiles. She couldn't believe she was getting a second chance.

"Gary, Roderick just called. He wants to meet with me tomorrow to talk."

Gary, smirking uncontrollably, said, "Oh yeah, we are about to get paid. You know, they just announced that Roderick is being considered as the number-one draft pick."

April, now disgusted, got up and walked away. Gary didn't even notice. He was old and decrepit. He was sixty but looked eighty. What April saw in him was beyond anyone's comprehension. Maybe, she was looking for that father figure, or she was just desperate for someone to take care of her.

Early in the morning, Laszlo arrived at Roderick's apartment to fit him with a wire. He did not mention Gary.

It was a precaution that Laszlo advised him to take just in case April slipped up and said something that would set Roderick off. It was still a sore topic. This meeting was to make April feel at ease to be able to have a conversation without taking off. Roderick's intention was for this to be over and done with. The baby's due date was in two weeks. This meeting would be taped while Laszlo listened.

April was all belly. Her petite frame waddled toward Roderick. Like a gentleman, he stood to give her a chair. He had loved her once and would have given her the world, but she crushed that dream. April was confident in her walk. A few eyes recognized her, but they quickly looked away when they saw she was pregnant. April didn't care how people perceived her. She was going to get paid.

Roderick pulled out a chair for her. He hugged her, but she wanted more.

"I just want to talk to you about how things are going. We need to come up with a plan for our child. I know I was being a jerk, but I am ready to take responsibility for our son or daughter. I don't want to know the sex of our baby. I want it to be a surprise."

"That's fine." Roderick played along. "I like surprises—good ones."

"I want to apologize. I never meant for any of this to happen." It was a partial truth. Her scheme was to get money and run, but a baby was not in the plan.

"Even if you and I don't agree with the circumstances, I do want us to be able to communicate and be good parents to our child," Roderick said nonchalantly.

April was afraid and an emotional wreck. She had to excuse herself to the restroom. What am I supposed to do? she thought. He's the father of this baby. Am I really this heartless and cold? Yes. I want what I want, and nothing is going to change that. She returned to the table confident that she would get all she expected from this situation.

"Roderick, I am willing to go forward, and I hope we can at least be friends."

"Of course. I hope so as well. I would like to be there when the baby is born."

"Sure. I will be delivering at UCLA." April knew what was coming next and beat him to the punch. "Right now, I don't want you to know where I live."

"Well, that's okay for now. I know that you have moved on. I'm not looking to stop by or anything, but eventually, I'm going to need to know where you live once the baby is born so that I can come visit."

"Well, we will worry about that when the time comes."

Their conversation ended there, and Roderick's plan was officially in motion.

~

Two weeks after their meeting, Roderick received a phone call from UCLA Hospital. He let the answering machine record the message. It was April.

"Roderick, this is April. I am at the hospital. If you want to be here, you'd better hurry."

Roderick made it to the hospital, hoping his father was there so he could confront him, but he wasn't. The nurse looked at him and smiled. "You young people just don't know what you are getting yourselves into. Sheesh!"

The nurse walked out of the room. Surprisingly enough, April was glad to see Roderick come through the door, but that happiness quickly diminished when Erica walked in behind him. Erica said nothing but hello and "God bless you" to her and made facial expressions that read I told you so and You'll never be able to pull anything on me, little girl. Erica walked out and sat in the waiting room. April was in too much pain to complain about her being there.

Roderick sat next to April on the bed when the doctor came in. "You are now six centimeters. We need to move you to the

birthing room."

Judging by her screams, you'd never know April was given an epidural an hour before. The doctor told April that it was time to push. Roderick was smiling from ear to ear as the head was crowning. "Wow," Dr. Stafford said. "Push once more, April, and this will

be over. Just one gigantic push, but when I tell you to stop, I need you to stop pushing."

Between breaths, April said okay.

After the last push, Dr. Stafford held the baby on the table so that Roderick could cut the umbilical cord.

While Roderick was inside, Erica was outside giving the court paperwork to the RN so that the investigator could take a DNA sample from the baby and Roderick.

The next day, Roderick and Mr. Rokowsky were staking out the hospital for any signs of Gary. He finally graced the hospital with his presence, but Roderick and Mr. Rokowsky didn't go in right away. They wanted him to get comfortable.

Roderick called the room to let April know he would stop by the next day instead so she would feel comfortable with Gary staying longer in the room.

Thirty minutes into Gary's visit with April, Roderick and Mr. Rokowsky showed up. Gary was taking a nap in the chair while April fed Roderick, Jr. She did a double take and seeing Roderick and Gary in the same room consumed her with fear.

"What is my father doing here, April? And you better not lie." April started squawking like a canary. "It was your father's idea." Gary woke up and quickly jumped to his feet.

"This was all about the money!" April shouted. "At first, I was supposed to make you fall in love with me. We were supposed to get married, and then I would leave you. But I got pregnant, which was not in the plan."

"Shut up, April," Gary said.

"No, I won't shut up this time. I knew we'd get caught eventually, and I'm glad we did."

Gary's rage was immeasurable. He put his hands around April's neck and began to choke her.

Roderick swung at Gary, knocking him off of April. As Gary stood up slowly, he was stunned for a minute and grabbed his jaw, which made it convenient for Mr. Rokowsky to put him in hand- cuffs. He sat him on the floor until the police could get there and arrested him for attempted murder.

Twenty minutes later, Erica arrived with Johnston. They had no idea what had transpired. Roderick's attorney was already there, interviewing April.

"Unfortunately for you," the attorney said to April, "we are pressing charges against you as well."

"What do you mean pressing charges against me?" April said. "I told the truth."

"It's for conspiracy to commit extortion with a minor." Roderick chimed in. "If I were you, I'd plead guilty."

April became indignant and didn't really understand the serious nature of the crime. "Gary will never testify against me; he loves me."

Roderick was disgusted by this notion.

"Well, if that's love, then I sure wouldn't want to be part of that kind of love. Besides, we don't need Gary's testimony. This was all taped, and we have you admitting to committing this crime with my father involved. And please, don't expect me to bring the baby to see you. I might consider monitored visits when you get out if you truly have changed your ways. I hear prison can really humble you or turn you into a psycho."

April began to cry. She knew she had no leg to stand on. "You can't do this to me. I'm the baby's mother."

Roderick felt pity for her and allowed her to see the baby one last time. She was his mother; he had compassion for that reason only, but he would never trust her again.

"April, do you think that I would even trust you with our son? You were so hell-bent on trying to get all you could from me, you were willing to use the baby to get it and more. You put your trust in my father and money instead of looking to God to supply all your needs. Ugh. Anyway, you slept with my father! Here's what I will do. If it turns out that the baby is my father's, I will keep him until you get out. I will love him like a brother should. If he is my son, I am going to ask for full custody. We should know the result of the paternity test in a couple of days. I am sorry it has to be this way, but God don't like ugly. While you are in jail and stripped of your freedom, I suggest you take that time to seek counsel, unconditional counsel, from the Almighty God. By then I pray that you would have understood what you've done."

Roderick had faced demonic people and forces of nature before. God allowed him to live and withstand kidnapping and torture, but this was beyond him.

~

Erica had been with Roderick for two months and was now back in Georgia.

"Mom, I don't know what to do with a baby. I am about to pull my hair out."

Erica laughed as loud as she could. Johnston could hear her all the way upstairs.

"Roderick, the baby is only two months old. He is going to cry and do all kinds of things that you are going to discover is wonderful. Enjoy him. If you are stressed, the baby can sense that. You need to relax. Hold him for a while, and once he goes to sleep, place him in the crib."

Roderick had frustration in his voice, and he was visibly afraid of his newborn son. He tried to convince his mother to come out to California two weeks earlier than she had planned.

"Mom, can you please come out earlier?"

"Roderick, I just left you a week ago. I have a home and a husband to take care of. I showed you everything, now you just have to trust yourself and be Jr.'s father. Also, you won't start training camp for four months, so you are going to have to suck it up and take care of your son. Plus, I have a job I haven't retired from yet. Besides, Marie will be there to help you out for a couple of days. You make sure your room is straight for her to sleep in."

At this point, Roderick was not going to complain. He was going to get extra help with the baby.

~

Back in Georgia, Greg was in his second year toward earning a PhD and finally found someone who was smarter than he was. He had fallen in love with a girl named Natasha.

"Natasha, I want you to meet my parents. They are great." "Greg, do you think they'll like me?"

"As long as I like you, you have nothing to worry about. Oh! By the way, you don't know a man named Gary, do you?"

"No. Why?"

"Well, I guess I better pull all the skeletons out of the closet."

Greg talked about his father and what his family had gone through. He made the long story short, but it still took four hours to tell it.

~

Back in California, both April and Gary were sitting in their jail cells, unable to comprehend the mess they had made of their lives to get rich. They both would be sitting behind bars for the next ten to fifteen years. Although April was able to contact her parents, they did not come to California to see her, but they did make the trip to see their grandson. Gary had no family members who would come to see him. He was lost and had truly become a miserable, old soul.

To be continued

A Call To Discipleship

If you have finished reading this book and want to know how to have a relationship with God, then open your Bibles and find the scriptures mentioned in this section. God's Word is true. If you seek Him, you will find Him. You may ask yourself, "How can I know God?" You can know the true and living God through His Word (the Bible, the Holy Scriptures).

It took me a long time to know that the Holy Scriptures reveal who God is and His plan for mankind before the beginning of time. It is through reading God's Word that we come to the knowledge and understanding of the righteousness of God and what He requires of us. But it is not just for our reading. We apply God's Word to our lives for God to work in and through us. That was the lesson Roderick had to learn, and many of us today still need to learn this truth.

We were created to have a loving relationship with God and to worship Him in spirit and truth. He is patiently and lovingly waiting for you to respond to His invitation to salvation and to say yes to His will. You too can receive forgiveness for your sins and assurance of eternal life through faith in our heavenly father and His only son, the Lord Jesus Christ (John 3:16–17 and John 17:3).

Why is it so hard for us to know God personally? It's hard because a lot of times we don't see ourselves like God sees us. Or once He reveals to us who we are, we deny the truth and don't want to acknowledge our own failures. Our sin separates us from God (Romans 3:23). Man was created to have fellowship with God, but because of sin (i.e., anything that is against the righteousness revealed in God's commandments), man was separated from that fellowship.

This means that anything less than being obedient to God's commands lead us out of fellowship with Him because God's Word says that obedience is better than sacrifice. There is no little or big sin. Sin is sin. April and Gary had to learn this also.

The ultimate result of sin is death and eternal damnation. Sin forces a separation from God. Man is sinful and God is holy. God said, "Be ye holy, for I am holy." The only solution is a divine bridge, and that bridge is Christ.

Jesus paid the price for us when he died on the cross (Romans 5:8). Christ's passionate, unconditional love and forgiving nature took on our burden of sin, which allows us to enter into that desired fellowship if we are obedient to His word and His way. He is the only way (John 14:6).

It's not just enough that you know these truths. We must repent of our sins and believe in Christ. We can know God personally and experience His love (John 1:12) and fight to the finish. You can receive Jesus Christ right now by faith (Romans 10:9–10).

If you now believe in God and have accepted Christ as your Lord and personal Savior, then know that heaven is rejoicing. You are welcomed into God's family. Remember, your new life has just begun. You have taken a leap of faith, and you must trust God with your whole heart, mind, and soul. Trials and unpleasant circumstances will come because our faith will to be tested and tried.

Also, remember that you now have an advocate in Jesus Christ, and he said that he would put no more on us than we can bear. Take all your addictions, your past hurts, unforgiveness, sorrow and pain, and leave them at the feet of Jesus. He will now carry your burdens for you. Please do not pick them up again. Obedience to God will be less of a burden and more of a joy to do.

Now that you are a Christian, you may wonder, "What now?" The true Christian faith recommends for believers, new and old, to find a church so that you hear the preaching of the Word and rejoice in the fellowship of other Christians. You must study the Bible because that is where we learn God and His plans. You have to pray for God to strengthen your faith and increase your love toward Him, and this will increase your love and compassion for others. Finally, seek after the Holy Spirit (the comforter) and enjoy the blessings given by God.

If you have any questions, search the scriptures, ask your pastor or someone who is faithful and strong in the Lord, and please do not lean on your own understanding. When we lean on our own understanding, we take God out of the equation. We need Him to lead and guide our lives daily. God said in His Word that *"Our thoughts are not His thoughts, and our ways are not His ways"* (Isaiah 55:8). Turn your wills over to God, and He will direct your path.

About the Author

The passion to write started in high school, and in her early twenties, experiencing vivid dreams, Amethyst in Love and Detective Brenda Sayers: Mercy Undercover (unpublished) were born. In 2016, she created Nita Nae's Books—Truthful Imagination to feed the imagination of readers. There were many dreams that followed, which generated other books, such as Apocalyptic 7: Salvation's Cry, birthed from a dream during her writing alluded to in Unconditional Counsel. Six novels have since followed—The Ghosts of Slavery's Dance, Unconditional Counsel 2: Fate Unbroken, Apocalyptic 8: Angels' of Heaven's Army, The Container, Opposing Fruit, and co-authorship for Embrace the Dawn: To Live Again with Margo Leonard (my mom—unpublished).

Arnita Renée—Nita Nae—was born and raised and yet lives in Los Angeles, California, where she accepted Christ at twenty-four. She earned a bachelor's degree in business management in 2002 and in 2007, a master's in justice administration. Arnita is a twenty-three- year veteran of Social Service Administration and Management and a seven-year Auditor II with the Los Angeles Police Department. Arnita serves on the Board of Trustees as treasurer, praise team and choir member at Greater Deliverance Church, in Inglewood, California.

The saga continues with Roderick, and the rest of his family living their lives as we left them. The Hawks drafted Roderick to the NBA as a first-round pick. He's come into his own as a father and well-rounded player as his first season ends, but has no love life. Drama continues when he finds a new love, Gary requests his presence and Aprils' release from prison is not far away. New and old characters emerge as his relationship blossoms and threatens to disrupt everything he has built. His priority is Roderick Jr., and the fight is on to keep him safe.

Other Books

Amethyst In Love, (KDP, 2019, eBook only)
Apocalyptic 7—Salvations Cry (Lulu.com, 2021, rev. 2025)
Embrace the Dawn to Live Again (Amazon, 2025)
The Ghosts of Slavery's Dance (Lulu.com, 2025)
Det. Brenda Sayers: Mercy Undercover (Lulu.com, 2025)

Future Books

Unconditional Counsel 2 – Fate Unbroken!
Apocalyptic 12—Angels of Heavens' Armies
The Container
Opposing Fruit
The Heart of an Untold Legacy: A Father's Story

Nita Nae's Books

Visit www.nitanaesbooks.com to order your signed copy.

Follow Me on Social Media:
FB: nitanaesbooks
IG: nitanaesbooks
Twitter: NitaNaesBooks
Pinterest: nitanaesbooks

For Author interviews and book information:
NNB Author's P.O.V. BLOG | nitanaesbooks.com
YouTube Channel https://youtu.be/OePi-LCJz_A

www.ingramcontent.com/pod-product-compliance
Lightning Source LLC
Chambersburg PA
CBHW072355030726

47505CB00014B/1842